Beware of Railway-Journeys

FRANK HELLER

Translated by Robert Emmons Lee

KABATY PRESS
Published by Kabaty Press, Warsaw
www.kabatypress.com

Introduction Copyright © Mitzi H. Brunsdale 2022

Editing and Project Management by Isobelle Clare Fabian

ISBN: 978-83-964260-0-0(Paperback)
       978-83-964260-3-1 (Hardcover)
       978-83-964260-1-7 (ePub)
       978-83-964260-2-4(PDF)

Cover Design © Jennifer Woodhead 2022

Interior Design and Typesetting: Minhajul Islam

Table of Contents

Introduction

S weden boasts Scandinavia's largest and most diverse population, which is reflected in the diversity of its crime fiction. Sparsely populated Norrland often engenders characters conditioned by a brutal northern climate, while central Svealand provides agricultural settings, and heavily populated southern Götaland offers urban political corruption, drug dealing, and criminal revenge in the capital city of Stockholm. Hakon Nesser, one of today's most distinguished practitioners of the genre, notes that "If you read 10 Swedish crime writers, you'll see that we're all very, very different," arguably a result of the country's varied geography and the diverse cultural elements affecting it throughout its history.

Unlike the Danish and Norwegian Vikings who ravaged Europe during the Middle Ages, Swedish seamen combined raiding with trading, primarily to the south. They brought home wealth and foreign cultural elements from far-off exotic places like Kievan Russia, Byzantium, and even Baghdad. Later, through participation in the Hanseatic League of traders, Swedes assimilated northern German cultural elements, especially in language and technology. After Sweden's Gustav I defeated the Hanseatic League in 1537, Sweden began to emerge from cultural isolation and harsh Lutheran strictures to absorb progressive ideas from Germany, France, Holland, and Italy.

By the early 1800s, however, Swedes were suffering agricultural failures and famine, unsettling political unrest, and a sense of national impotence. Led by their newspapers, notably Stockholm's *Aftonbladet,* Sweden's middle class demanded political reforms and got them around 1840.

At the same time Swedish readers, after enduring a generally indigestible diet of Lutheranism and otherworldly New Romantic poetry, began to seek out realistic fiction. One of Sweden's first crime novels, *The Mariner's Wife: A True Story*, featuring a crime and its solution, appeared in 1837. Meanwhile, a new Swedish journalistic style was becoming popular, described by Alric Gustafson as "concrete, direct, factual, and when necessary sharp, invidious, even brutal." With economic and political problems at home, by the 1880s over one per cent of Sweden's population annually emigrated to the United States, while many of those who stayed home developed a taste for the short realistic stories *Aftonbladet* was publishing. As Bruce Murphy has observed, "people like to read about what's bothering them . . . heightened anonymity, social insecurity, and urban poverty are like fertilizer for criminality."

At the same time, an influx of classic English, French, and American crime fiction authored in the 1800s began to appear in Swedish translation. Many involved a "Great Detective" figure, notably Arthur Conan Doyle's Sherlock Holmes, Edgar Allan Poe's Auguste Dupin and figures in the German horror tales of E.T.A. Hoffman. They inspired Carl Jonas Love Almqvist, considered the father of Swedish detective fiction and Fredrik Lindholm, whose *The Stockholm Detective* is Sweden's first full-length crime novel. For a long time, the Swedish literary establishment denounced crime fiction as "vulgar trash" and "dirt literature," and non-Swedes know very little about the earliest Swedish crime writers.

Starting in the 1920s, however, Americans knew one early Swedish crime author. From 1914 until he died in 1947, Gunnar Serner, writing as "Frank Heller," produced 43 crime novels and many short stories and travelogues, making him probably the first Swedish crime writer translated into English and the internationally most successful Swedish entertainment author of his time. In 1923, just as his deliciously humorous novel *The Emperor's Old Clothes* was appearing in New York, Heller gave *Everybody's Magazine*'s Chimney Corner section an amusing account of the birth of his writing career. After he went to break the bank in Monte Carlo, he emerged with only twenty francs in his pocket. He had "cut most of the cables" connecting him "with the land of Charles X," and also being wanted by the Stockholm police for forgery, he "had to find a way of whiling away both time and, which was even more important, appetite."

Heller found it: writing crime fiction. In 1923, he contributed his first of a series of stories to *Everybody's Magazine,* describing the "new central character" of "Mr. Collin's Adventures" as a Raffles-type "international swindler of singular cunning and most noble heart," a detective and a thief. As a novel, *Mr. Collin's Adventures* became an international hit translated into several languages, launching Heller's long career. He wrote, ". . . from the day of its publication to now [1923] neither world wars nor revolutions have stopped my moving finger." The engaging Mr. Collin reappeared in several popular novels published in English in the 1920s.

K. Arne Blom believed that French crime writers influenced Heller's work more than Sherlock Holmes, despite the allusions to the latter in Heller's stories. Blom thought Philip Collin was primarily inspired by Maurice Leblanc's thief-detective Arsène Lupin, a master of disguise who operated a criminal ring with a large-town sized budget and who liked to humiliate the police, even masquerading for four years as the head of the Sûreté. Heller adapted factors of Lupin's *modus operandi* to often riotous use in a novel markedly different from the Collin books, *The Marriage of Yussuf Khan* (retitled in this edition as *Beware of Railway-Journeys*), also published in New York in 1923. It has a slyly satiric style that punctures the foibles of nationally diverse upper-crust echelons of Roaring Twenties society.

Heller made Allan Krogh, the hero of *Beware of Railway-Journeys,* a somewhat naïve young Swede and gave him a youthful predicament like Heller's own. Having blown through his university funds, Allan has Swedish creditors at his heels, so he is seeking adventure in Europe—and he finds it. One lovely September day he impetuously takes a German train speeding from Hamburg to Paris, after being smitten by a haughty young grey-eyed American woman he sees buying a ticket. Poor Allan can't help himself being drawn into a series of mishaps involving near-caricatures of various nationalities, starting with his arrest in Cologne, where bumptious German policemen accuse him of being the notorious super-swindler Benjamin Mirzl, wanted for an immense jewel theft in Berlin.

His mishaps continue in London's Grand Hotel Hermitage, where he meets stereotypically loud and tasteless but well-meaning Americans Mr. and Mrs. Bowlby and their husband-seeking daughter Helen. He learns that Yussuf Khan, a young maharajah, is coming there with a blimpish British colonel as babysitter, a household imam spouting verses from Omar the Tentmaker, and a fortune in jewels, seeking an English bride—and that grey-eyed beauty is also on the prowl. A series of entanglements fueled by sundry libations ensues. Frequently asking himself what the Great Detective would do, Allan blunders into the solution of one crisis after another, all orchestrated by the mysterious multiple-disguised Mirzl. Throughout this novel, Heller's light but realistic and factual touch, an eye for historically detailed and scrumptiously concrete settings, and well-rounded humorous but sympathetic characters make this international caper still enjoyable reading today. K. Arne Blom summed up Heller's position in Swedish letters succinctly: among the pedestrian Swedish crime authors of his time, Heller was simply "a virtuoso," "a crane among sparrows."

—Mitzi M. Brunsdale

CHAPTER I

BEWARE OF
RAILWAY-JOURNEYS!

"Diner, meine Herrschaften! Wünschen die Herrschaften zu dinieren? Diner, meine Herrschaften; zweite Service jetz fertig!"

As the steward's call for dinner service echoed along the carriages, the train was speeding along the shining steel rails on its way to Cologne. The railway carriages swayed as they passed over the curves, leaning first to one side, then to the other. The landscape flew by, flat and uninteresting; Osnabrück had been left behind a couple of hours before. The September sky was of a clear blue, endlessly high with its masses of shining white clouds pursuing each other; the wind was fresh and cool, already bringing with it a slight but perceptible scent of autumn. Now and then a stream or canal flew past, the water a transparent green, with here and there an early fallen leaf sailing over the surface. The train sped on and on; Allan Kragh, his head partly stretched out of a window in the corridor, stood quietly thinking, never minding the wind which was beating against his face, nor the occasional gust of cinders from the locomotive. The voice of the waiter from the restaurant car aroused him from his thoughts; he looked at his watch, saw it was a little after one, and suddenly remembered that he had eaten nothing since the two eggs and coffee at the Central Station in Hamburg. As he remembered this fact, he also realized that he was in possession of an excellent appetite. He motioned to the man with the white jacket and received a card entitling him to a place in the restaurant car.

"Each serving of dinner is full up to-day," this worthy confided to Allan, as though discreetly hinting that a tip would not be out of place later on.

"Have they begun to serve dinner?" asked Allan.

"They will start in two minutes, mein Herr."

The envoy from the restaurant car hurried away and Allan went lurching down the corridor to the washroom at the end of the carriage.

The reasons for Allan being on board this particular train are not easy to explain, or more correctly speaking, the one and only reason was so bizarre that it sounds ridiculous to mention it. He had left his native Sweden in search of adventure, as well as to preserve his remaining capital, which had shown a wonderful facility of slipping out through the gratings to the bank cashier's window during several eventful years of university life. Early that September morning he had arrived in Hamburg without the slightest idea as to which way he should steer his course or what he should do next. Taking a short walk at random through the streets on that side of the station where the incoming trains arrived, he found himself, after strolling about for a short time, down by the Alster. For a time he speculated upon and considered the idea of remaining for a while in Hamburg, which seemed to him a beautiful and attractive city. Then he gave up the idea and returned to the railway station through the still-empty streets of early morning (it was but a little after seven). The station, he found, provided all modern conveniences; he had a shave, changed some Swedish money, and ate a hasty breakfast in the large restaurant. At five minutes before half-past seven an attendant in a gold-bedecked uniform announced a train for Paris; Allan left the restaurant, still without a definite idea as to what he intended to do, and went toward the ticket windows. Timetables covered the walls in orderly columns like so many troops of soldiers; no placards with tempting pictures of blue seas and green woods, nothing but printed notices and series of numbers. At one of the through-ticket windows stood three persons who suddenly drew Allan's attention: a young man, perhaps thirty, of about his own height, who looked like an actor with his dark-complexioned, clean-shaven upper lip and chin, short side-whiskers and gold-rimmed pince-nez; an old gentleman with a red hawk-like nose, yellowish-gray mustache, and piercing yellow eyes betraying the drinker; and thirdly a young lady in a green travelling costume, open at the neck and closely fitting over the hips, with skirt short enough to reveal two buttoned shoes and gray gaiters. Her face had a somewhat haughty expression, with her two large gray eyes and rather short upper lip, and was extremely striking beneath the travelling hat of black and green which rested like a musketeer's cap on her reddish-blonde hair. She carried three or four American magazines in her hand. Allan devoured her with his eyes; she could have been d'Artagnan's lady-love or one of the Cardinal's beautiful blonde agents. Now the young man hurried away from the ticket-window; the older man took his place, closely followed by the striking young woman who held some gold pieces between her gloved fingers. The older man left and she took his place. A thought struck Allan and he moved into line behind her. He heard her say in perfectly correct German:

"First class, single ticket, Paris."

She asked a couple of questions which the man behind the window answered. She was German, then, although she looked the typical American. Now she received her ticket. Allan left the window and followed her at a distance. He saw her register some luggage and then go down the steps to the platform. She appeared even more attractive, moving in her free, elastic way, than she had when standing still. He could see her, down below, walking the length of the train; then she disappeared. The attendant in the gold-bedecked uniform came wandering through the station and shouted in the voice of a drill sergeant:

"Train for Paris and Holland! Leaves in one minute!"

It was then that a wild idea came into Allan's head. Without further thought at what he was doing or why he did it, he rushed back to the ticket-window where he had seen the three, pulled out a bank-note and shrieked at the man inside, who had stared at him before when he had left the window without getting a ticket:

"Paris, single ticket, first class!"

"You will have to hurry!" yelled the man in return. "The train leaves at 7:39—you have only forty seconds left!"

Allan rushed away with the ticket in his hand and confused thoughts flying through his head. Why, this was nothing but pure madness. His luggage had been placed in the check-room; it was out of the question to get it and take it with him on the same train; he really should give up this hare-brained idea—or should he leave his bags and trunk here and telegraph for them later? The whole thing was crazy. . . there were other trains later. . . but she was going on this one! If he should be lucky enough to tell her of his sacrifice for her sake, then perhaps she would feel pleased and flattered. Without knowing how, he was through the gate, rushing head over heels down the stairs to a train which was on the point of starting, the guards shutting the last doors with a slam—it was then, just at the last moment, that with one jump he landed in one of the rear carriages. Safely on board he again hesitated a moment. It was nothing but pure madness! Should he jump off again? Then he shrugged his shoulders and laughed to himself.

"If I go ahead," he murmured confidentially to the corridor-window, "I will at least avoid having to pay a fine for breaking the law by jumping off a train in motion."

After he had made sure that he was in the last carriage for passengers, he started along the corridor in search of the fair unknown.

He had entered a third class carriage which he went through without paying attention to its occupants. After that followed a second class carriage bound for Amsterdam, which was so full of passengers that he forced his way along with some difficulty. Then came a direct carriage for Southern Germany, nearly filled. The next was the restaurant car. Here he was not allowed to pass because he would have to go through the kitchen. Allan tried bribes, which were refused, and he was informed he would have to wait until Bremen, where the train stopped a minute. He settled down to rest at a window in the corridor of the carriage going to Southern Germany, where he let himself be permeated with the morning sunshine and drank in his share of the cool September air. He threw out his chest and laughed to himself; this was something different than trudging along the worn streets of that provincial Sybaris that was his university town. Suddenly the railway carriages began to bump against each other, the train slowed down and after rolling by a suburb with red-tiled villas, came into Bremen. Quick as a flash Allan was out in the station, bought a package of cigarettes, some fruit and a few newspapers, and hurried back to the coach just in front of the restaurant car which before had obstructed his progress.

He waited until the train started before he resumed his search. This time it was crowned with the greatest of success. It turned out that the carriage in front of the one he had entered was for first and second class passengers, and ran direct to Paris; in the third compartment of the first class part sat the fair unknown.

Unfortunately she was not alone. The old gentleman with the red hawk-like nose and the matted yellowish-gray mustache sat opposite her at the window; she was riding backwards, he in the direction the train was going. They seemed to be unacquainted with each other. Allan looked hesitatingly into the compartment for a moment; the old gentleman with the fine red-wine nose had encumbered the rack on his side with a mass of luggage—suitcases, Gladstone bags, travelling rugs, field-glass cases, and the Lord knows what—all of which stood in proportion to his olfactory organ's respectable appearance.

The unknown opposite him had two small bags, a hat box and some travelling cushions. At the moment she was sitting sunk back in an artistically assumed pose between four of the latter, and seemed to be sleeping. Allan stared in wonder at her high-bred profile and the shadow which her eyelashes cast on her delicate cheeks; her reddish-blonde hair, thick and wavy, was slightly rumpled. The short travelling skirt had crept a trifle above her gray gaiters and gave a glimpse which proved that not only her ankle was slender and well-formed. After a couple of moments' hesitation he entered and sat down on the seat by the old gentleman.

The latter greeted his entrance with a look of hearty disgust. He turned his eyes up toward the rack as much as to say that if Allan (who could go to the devil as far as he was concerned) wanted to place (which the good Lord forbid) his unwelcome travelling effects up above, then he would be obliged to move his own property there deposited. Allan shrugged his shoulders in a manner which showed little less contempt for a fellow-traveller than had the gentleman with the red-wine nose, and which was intended to convey the information that he (who according to international agreements had full rights to travel in the class for which he had bought his ticket) through a whim preferred, while riding in that Prussian-Hessian railway-carriage, to let the check-room at the Central Station in Hamburg take charge of his hand luggage, luggage which could stand a rigid comparison with the travelling effects of even that old gentleman who had the deepest colored Bordeaux-nose on the whole train. After the exchange of their rapier-like glances both quietly settled down in their places; he with the hawk-like nose taking refuge behind the Hamburger *Fremdenblatt*, Allan remaining without shelter. The young lady's eyelashes, which for a couple of seconds had raised themselves slightly without anyone noticing it, again resumed their enchanting position over her cheeks.

The train whizzed on and the heavens shone bright in the September sunlight. Allan sank back into a vague, hazy reverie, his eyes wandering now and then to his vis-à-vis.

They were about halfway between Bremen and Osnabrück (it was around ten o'clock) when the guard suddenly put in an appearance for the purpose of examining the tickets, and giving each person a card reserving their seats for them. Allan handed over his ticket for examination; the old gentleman with the hawk-like nose did the same.

The fair unknown in the corner by the window apparently remained asleep. The guard gave an apologetic cough and in vain spoke to the "Gnädige" a couple of times. She did not stir. Allan thought he saw his opportunity. He leaned forward and lightly tapped that part of her green travelling suit where the rounding of her knee was indistinctly outlined. She opened her eyes, stared a second at Allan's hand, which he had not yet withdrawn, and straightened up with a look of such unmistakable repugnance that Allan started back, his whole face a deep red. The guard smiled discreetly and repeated his "Gnädige!" The fair unknown handed out her ticket, her eyes fixed on Allan as though she would like to murder him; then she suddenly changed from pantomime to speech. The words came in English—Allan felt a bit surprised since she had spoken such perfect German in the station at Hamburg. It was impossible for him to imagine that she could be anything but German. It was to the old gentleman with the hawk-like nose that she turned.

"Sir, I presume you understand my language? I don't speak yours."

"A lie," thought Allan, "but why?"

"I do speak English," said the old gentleman.

"Thank you. Do you know whether this young person here took any further liberties with me while I slept?"

The old gentleman gave Allan a dagger-like look and said:

"That I can't say. I have been reading my newspaper."

"Very well! Thank you!" She then burst out with a torrent of American indignation: Couldn't a lady travel alone on a train in Europe without being insulted by the first person who happened to come along?—were there no compartments reserved for ladies? —One would imagine that people who could afford to travel first class would be gentlemen.

The old gentleman listened to her with apparent approval. Allan, who scarcely realized whether he was asleep or awake, began to stammer an explanation.

"Madame, let me try to explain. . ."

"How *dare* you speak to me!" she cried.

This was too much for Allan. He arose with the most ironical air he could assume—he realized that his cheeks were still red from surprise and indignation—and making a bow in a most subservient manner, said:

"Allow me to correct you in one point, Madame. If you wish to avoid further contact with gentlemen like me there is nothing to prevent you: the next compartment is reserved for ladies."

With as much dignity as a person can command when loaded down with a cane, four newspapers and a package of fruit, he left the compartment. A long icy-cold "im-per-ti-nence" from the unknown pierced his back like a final stab. But in spite of it all Allan was not at all sure that he had not got the best of her.

The first person he spied in the corridor was, to his surprise, none other than the third of the trio he had seen at the ticket-window in Hamburg—the dark-complexioned man with the side-whiskers and gold-rimmed pince-nez, the man who looked like an actor. As Allan moved from the doorway of the compartment he had a momentary impression that this gentleman had observed the entire scene within and that an almost imperceptible smile trembled around the corners of his mouth. But the next moment his eyes were directed straight ahead through the open door to his own compartment, absorbed in admiration of the moors, stretching into the far distance outside. Allan glanced at him quickly as he went by him down the corridor. The other compartments of the railway carriage were all more or less occupied with exception of the one reserved for ladies, concerning which he had just imparted to the fair unknown the information of its existence. He turned back to where the man with the gold-rimmed pince-nez was standing in the corridor before the entrance to his compartment, and made a slight gesture toward the open door.

"May I?"

"Certainly."

He who looked like an actor nodded politely. Allan went in, threw himself back on the unoccupied seat and lit a cigarette after carefully convincing himself that he was in a smoking compartment.

What a shameless little devil of a vixen! The deuce

take all such Americans! And further, the devil take him himself and all other idiots who start out on all so-called adventurous expeditions lured on by such will-o'-the-wisps. And finally the devil take him again for journeying away from his luggage in Hamburg simply to have abuse showered upon him by such a pretty, shameless little devil of a vixen. . .

His peevish humor lasted for a couple of hours. The train whizzed on its way toward Osnabrück stopping for a couple of moments in that city famous for the treaty of peace once signed there; it rushed along toward Cologne; people wandered into the restaurant car to refresh themselves with its German twelve-o'clock dinner. Among others he saw the American and the old gentleman with the hawk-like nose go strolling in, now in animated conversation; but Allan had lost interest in the whole affair. The September air, which before had been clear and blue like the air should be in time of adventure, was now cold and with a repellent tinge; the sun was without warmth. The gentleman with the pince-nez came into the compartment and became absorbed in the study of an illustrated catalogue; now and then he cast a surreptitious glance at Allan, who every time returned it with a defiant stare. Finally Allan went out in the corridor and had stayed there with his head half out of the window for some three quarters of an hour when the drummer up of trade for the restaurant car aroused him from his bad humor with his: "Wünschen die Herrschaften zu dinieren?" He quickly washed up and went through the corridors to the restaurant car.

When he reached the carriage next his own, he received a little shock; the hot-headed American was just returning through the corridor, in lady-like manner balancing herself to the swayings of the train. Behind her the Bordeaux-nosed old gentleman, with the olfactory organ shining brighter than ever, could indistinctly be seen; in his mouth was a freshly lighted Havana, the red glow from which shone but dimly by the side of the said organ. Allan hastily stepped aside into one of the compartments to let the pair pass; but as the young lady went by he could not avoid catching a glance from her gray eyes—but oh, wonder! Had he seen aright? Her eyes now seemed almost friendly with the faintest bit of a smile glimmering deep within. She swept by with a rustle of silk skirts. The old gentleman, whose eyes had taken on a satisfied Sultan-like shimmer, rolled on close behind her, with never a look for Allan or, as a matter of fact, for anything but the American's slender willow-like waist. Allan stared at them and then gave a start as at the end of the corridor he noticed the man who looked like an actor, gazing at the two with an infinitesimal smile glimmering through his gold-rimmed pince-nez. Allan watched him for a moment and then continued on his way.

Nearly all seats in the restaurant car were taken; at the further end next to the kitchen a table for two was still unoccupied. The aforementioned white-jacketed drummer-up of trade motioned from the distance with his napkin as though to impress on Allan that it was only with the greatest of difficulty he had been able to reserve a place for him at that table. Allan sat down, looked over the menu with its five-syllabled German names and then passed on to the wine list. He had just reached the conclusion that Graacher Auslese was a suitable wine for a journey on a September day when someone took the seat opposite him. He glanced up. With illogical surprise he recognized in his table companion the man with the gold-rimmed pince-nez.

This gentleman gave Allan a smile of recognition and then began to gaze out of the window. Allan for a while watched the waiter's balancing act as he passed between the tables with plates and dishes; each time the train swung around a curve and he himself was thrown to one side by the motion, he felt a queer sensation in the pit of his stomach, and the thought would come to him: "Now for a crash!" But not even once did there come so much as a spot on the table cloth. Suddenly the waiter stood by his place with a plate of soup in his hand. Allan made an involuntary grimace and shook his head: soup at that time of day! The man with the pince-nez again smiled faintly as he dipped his spoon into his own plate of soup.

"You do not care for the German meals?" he asked.

"Lord help me, no."

"German wine is more to your taste?"

"Certain kinds. Perhaps you will have a glass with me?"

Allan's good humor quickly rose several degrees as soon as he had opened his mouth; he began to learn from experience that man is a companion-loving animal, even when bent on solitary adventure. The stranger made a slight bow.

"Gladly, if you will let me return the courtesy later."

Allan motioned the waiter to bring another glass. He and the stranger then drank to each other.

"You are a Scandinavian?"

"What makes you think so? Can you notice it by my speech?"

"Not exactly, but I can tell from your appearance and then besides there is something else which I cannot quite define. I'd even be willing to wager that you are either Swedish or Norwegian."

"Really?"

"The Danes can never learn to pronounce our 'a'—they always give a bleating sound to the letter. And since you do not do that, why, the question is solved!"

Allan nodded without confirming the stranger's hypothesis about his nationality. To be sure he was rather tall and slender, but since he was dark-complexioned that should not betray him, if his accent did not.

The man with the pince-nez, who had finished his soup, leaned forward and resumed the conversation. Allan studied his face, which showed energy and intelligence; those eyes behind the lenses of the pince-nez did not seem at all weakened through near-sightedness. It was undeniably a sympathetic face. Once, as the man burst into a laugh from some remark he himself had made, Allan quickly noticed that one of his lower teeth was capped with gold. Queerly enough this slight blemish engraved itself on his memory, as such small matters often do; and although at the moment he hardly thought further about it—yet it was to prove of more importance on a later occasion than he could possibly imagine.

Suddenly he noticed that he had been so preoccupied watching the stranger that he had forgotten to listen to what he had to say; he started as he heard the word Paris uttered in a questioning tone of voice, and hastily assumed that his table-companion had asked when they were to arrive there.

"I don't know," he said.

The man with the gold-rimmed pince-nez looked at him in astonishment.

"You do not know whether you are going to Paris?" he asked. "This train goes there in any case, even if you don't know it!"

The desire suddenly came over Allan to boast about himself and what he had done earlier in the day.

"*That* I do know," he said seriously. "But on the contrary, I do not know whether I am going to Paris. I know as little about that as I know why I am travelling on this train anyway."

"You don't know why you are travelling on this train?"

"No, nor as a matter of fact, why I'm travelling at all."

"Donnerwetter! Do you mean to say that you are in the habit of stepping on to an express train without knowing where it is going?"

"I happened to do so this morning, at least."

"Donnerwetter! May I inquire whether you find time to

do much packing when you travel in this way?"

"Not this morning, I must admit—in the rush I was obliged to leave my luggage in Hamburg."

And with an indifference worthy of a Phileas Fogg Allan waved the red check from the Central Station at Hamburg in the air. 374 was printed on it in heavy black type. The stranger stared at the piece of paper and at Allan with an air of respect, which under the circumstances was extremely flattering, and after another "Donnerwetter!" emptied his glass of Rhine wine at a gulp; Allan refilled it with the feelings of a Mæcenas. At that moment the fish course was brought in; after the man with the gold-rimmed pince-nez had let the waiter serve it, he continued the topic of conversation.

"Pardon me, if I appear inquisitive, but was it really only through mere caprice that you left your luggage behind and started off on a train with no particular reason for the journey?"

He looked intently at Allan, who just then was the object of the waiter's attention and for the moment seemed to have eyes for nothing but the food before him. A peculiar expression of excitement appeared in the eyes of the stranger; and if Allan had looked up he would have perceived how his vis-à-vis made a queer sort of grimace at the waiter, a thrusting out of his lips and two short shakes of his head in Allan's direction. But Allan had no eyes for the grimaces and he saw as little of what followed: the waiter hastily turned his head, stared at him and then raised his eyebrows questioningly to the man with the gold-rimmed pince-nez. He quickly formed a word with his lips which the waiter obviously understood for he raised his eyebrows still higher and for the first time during the entire dinner his hand trembled. This whole affair had hardly taken fifteen seconds. Allan, who was still debating with himself whether or not to tell his dinner companion of his episode with the unknown lady in Hamburg at last looked up.

"As a matter of fact, I did have a reason," he said, "for leaving my luggage in the lurch, but—well, I am afraid that I had better not attempt to tell you about it. But it was the same reason which caused me to take this express train and it is of rather too delicate a nature to mention."

The man with the gold-rimmed pince-nez was able to make another almost imperceptible gesture to the waiter, who paid close attention before he disappeared again with the dishes. Then lifting his glass, he said:

"It is my turn now. Do you prefer Bordeaux or Burgundy?"

They remained there some half hour after dessert, finishing their coffee, while the train rushed on through the clear autumn day. Allan became more and more interested in his travelling companion; he was an entertaining, striking sort of character, had evidently travelled, and was full of stories from every corner of Europe. Now and then he again mentioned his surprise at Allan's way of leaving his luggage behind on his journey, and Allan felt more and more satisfied with himself. Once his companion left the table for a couple of moments, and in the outer, empty part of the restaurant car exchanged a few words with the waiter without Allan especially noticing it or thinking anything about it. When he came back he began a story which, as he proceeded, confirmed Allan in his theory that the man was an actor; he even mentioned his name in passing—Ludwig Koch. Allan was just considering whether it would be the correct thing for him to introduce himself or not, when the train drew in to a large station, slowed up and stopped.

The man with the pince-nez turned toward the window and looked out while the train was slowing up at the platform. With his hand shielding his eyes he quickly glanced over the people on the platform; evidently he saw someone he knew for he gave a little cry as though of recognition, arose from his place, nodded to Allan and hurried out.

"Will be back in a moment!" he cried.

"Don't go off and leave your luggage as I did," Allan called after him in reply.

The man with the pince-nez disappeared without further remarks. To Allan's surprise, hardly fifteen seconds after he had gone the train started with a jerk and rolled out of the station without Allan noticing the name of the place, he was so occupied in peering out of the window after his companion at table. He saw no trace of him on the platform; he must therefore have jumped into one of the carriages further back. Allan turned his head towards the entrance to the restaurant car, ready to greet Mr. Koch with congratulations at his success in getting back on the train. But a couple of minutes went by, and Mr. Koch did not appear. Allan settled back again in his seat and began to look out at the landscape.

The train rushed on through a manufacturing district. Only high chimneys were to be seen, from which billows of dense smoke surged forth, forming long, slowly-moving belts across the blue sky, like strands of seaweed in the water; grayish yellow factory buildings; masses of sidings where dirty red boxcars stood clustered together. The grass and weeds were scanty and yellow as though parched with fever; piles of slags and cinders rose on high, like erupted ashes around a crater. The whole was depressing, dreary. To *live* in such surroundings, to be bound down for life in such a prison. . . Allan shuddered, looked up at the blue September sky, beckoning to adventure, glad that he was sitting in that railway carriage, rolling along with steady rhythmic motion, and quoted, half audibly and with feeling, four lines by Snoilsky which laid stress on the contrasts between a first class passenger and the locomotive engineer. Then happening to think of Mr. Koch again, he motioned to the waiter.

"Let me have my check, Ober. I will go back to my compartment and look for my friend."

The waiter's face twitched quickly, but with merely a "Sehr gut," he quickly scribbled some hieroglyphics on a piece of paper.

"Nine marks sixty pfennigs, bitte!"

Allan paid, and handed him a tip. Suddenly a thought

entered his head.

"But Mr. . . but the other gentleman?"

"He has already paid."

"Paid?"

"Jawohl, quite a while ago."

The waiter spoke in an absolutely indifferent tone of voice, and then hurried away as soon as he had answered. Allan suppressed a sudden feeling of surprise. Mr. Koch had paid! When? Was a person in the habit of paying here in the restaurant car before he had finished? And quietly, so no one would notice? As far as he was concerned, he had not seen Mr. Koch give the waiter a pfennig. He shrugged his shoulders and went back to his compartment so as to have a talk with Mr. Koch and find out what had happened. The train had again begun to sway and jolt, and it took a little time and some skill in balancing to make a way through the corridors, which now were almost empty. At one time the carriage gave such a heavy jounce as the train went by a junction at full speed that Allan was thrown right about; to his surprise, he noticed at the other end of the corridor no less a person than the restaurant waiter who seemed to be following him. However, at the very moment Allan looked at him, the man stepped aside into one of the compartments. Allan remembered that he might also be waiting on people in the compartments, and surmising that the fellow was on some such errand, continued on his way.

At last he had reached the railway carriage containing his compartment. He passed the coupé which the American and the old gentleman had appropriated and opened the sliding door to his own compartment. "Well, Mr. Koch, you didn't come back after all!" was on the tip of his tongue when he suddenly checked himself.

Mr. Koch was not in the compartment; it was empty.

Allan remained standing a moment in the doorway before he started to go in. What on earth was the matter! He certainly was not there. But his luggage . . there was no luggage there either! Only a very small handbag. Like lightning a thought flashed through his mind: no other luggage had been there when Mr. Koch had been in the compartment. Mr. Koch was travelling with almost as little as he himself. . . He was interrupted in these astounding reflections by the sound of quiet steps, almost on tip-toe, in the corridor. By the two-bearded Soliman, if there wasn't that restaurant car waiter again!

This time his presence there and his quick, wary, weasel-like glance into the compartment struck Allan as so unnecessary and downright peculiar that he jumped up from his seat and rushed out into the corridor to have a few words with this serving-brother of his. But he had already disappeared into the next carriage and Allan, with wrinkled brow, returned to his seat. For a few seconds he thought of hunting up the guard and consulting him about what could have happened to Mr. Koch; then he concluded to let the whole matter go to the deuce anyway—he didn't even know the fellow—and became absorbed in studying the only luggage, with exception of the diminutive handbag, which his travelling companion had left behind on the seat, namely an illustrated catalogue of magic tricks and illusions issued by a firm in Berlin.

It was about five o'clock when the train rolled into the station at Cologne, where Allan's first real adventure began. He never afterwards forgot the afternoon sunlight as it filtered in through the immense train-shed, shining like yellow girders through the clouds of dust and smoke. The broad platform was full of people swarming around news- and book-stands, around tiny stalls where beer, bananas and raisin-buns were sold. A fat old woman, who strikingly resembled a captive balloon swaying and tugging at its anchor rope, toddled along in her rôle of flower girl. Allan drew back from the window and stretched up his hand to the rack for his belongings—a hat and cane (his overcoat was still in Hamburg). He intended to go out and walk around a bit. He had just put his hat on his head when the figures of three men darkened the doorway of his compartment. The one preceding the others was quietly clad in a double-breasted civilian suit of blue; behind him, to Allan's unutterable surprise, appeared the white-jacketed waiter from the restaurant-car, and a huge German policeman in all his glory of helmet and sabre.

Allan's first impulse, as he stared at the trio, was to step back (which the reader under the same circumstances would also probably do); he had time to take one step, but no more, for evidently fearing he would jump out of the window, the man in civilian clothes rushed forward with the policeman at his side, and each laying a hand on Allan's shoulder cried in unison, as though repeating part of a litany:

"In the name of the law we arrest you!"

Allan was too stunned to think of resistance. The only thought he could formulate was, "What in the devil does it mean? Is it revenge on the part of my creditors back home? Have they asked these German sausage-eaters to send me back?" Then the man in civilian clothes (a soggy-complexioned individual with clammy hands, as Allan had reason to know) opened his mouth and said sneeringly:

"Don't look so amazed, my dear Benjamin Mirzl! We all know, Mr. Mirzl, that you are clever at disguising yourself, but there are people who can see through your little tricks. Come along without making a fuss. You don't need a porter to carry your luggage this time."

"Luggage? That isn't my bag," Allan managed to answer.

"Of course not! Ha! ha! Of course not!"

"My luggage is in Hamburg!" shouted Allan, with a vague presentiment of how the whole matter hung together beginning to dawn deep within him.

"Ha! ha! ha! Of course! Of course! But why not in St. Petersburg? Well, Mirzl, you are caught this time. Make the best of it, that is all you can do."

"My name isn't Mirzl, or what, zum Donnerwetter, you say it is. My name is Kragh and. . ."

"Stillschweigen!" roared the gigantic policeman, whose peace of mind was disturbed by the laurels being won by the man in civilian clothes. "Come along to the police station, and if you promise to go peaceably, I'll walk along behind you."

"But. . ." Allan began and then stopped; it wasn't worth-while to start protesting here. With a shrug of his shoulders he stepped into the corridor. The man in civilian clothes, carrying Mr. Koch's diminutive handbag, followed closely on his heels, and the mammoth policeman brought up the rear of the procession. Suddenly Allan heard the waiter cry out: "But my reward! Where do I apply for it?"

"That you will find out later!" the man in civilian clothes called back over his shoulder. "Moreover there are two of you in on that. The fellow who got off at Essen, you can be sure, won't let you have the whole of it."

With these words of the man in civilian clothes ringing in his ears, and with that worthy person himself by his side, followed by the huge guardian of the law, Allan passed by the pair in the other compartment—the American and the elderly gentleman with the hawk-like nose. He saw her raise her delicate eyebrows and excitedly whisper something to the old fellow—they were evidently bosom friends by now. He bowed his head so as to see no more and turned off to the right in the direction pointed out by the man in civilian clothes. *What* did it all mean? Adventure, adventure in September under a shining sun and in the clear blue open—why, this looked most of all like a total eclipse of the sun and mighty close air. What did it all *mean*?

No philosopher could more emphatically have asked himself the question.

* * *

"Is that your passport? You are Mr. Allan Kragh, student, Swedish citizen?"

Allan answered both of these questions in the affirmative with an emphasis which was only held within certain bounds through his fear of irretrievably offending the little fat police magistrate. A day and a half in that black hole!

"Why didn't you enter a protest with me before if that *is* your passport?"

Allan stared at the representative of the law and swallowed a few good plain Swedish expressions before he answered:

"From the first moment I have insisted on who I was, although your da. . . although no one would listen to me. It seemed to be proved with mathematical certainty that I must be Mirzl—may the devil take him, whoever Mirzl is! Mirzl! I've never heard about any Mirzl!"

"Then you don't read the newspapers very carefully or the papers in Sweden don't keep up with the times. Well, we'll make some inquiries by telegraph. If they prove to be in your favor, we will reconsider your case this very afternoon."

"I thank you most kindly, thank you *most.* . . "

"But I want to call your attention to the fact that the affair of the handbag makes us very wary. To be sure, it contains nothing really compromising, but it is known that Mirzl had such a bag in his possession when he disappeared from Berlin."

"The handbag! How often must I tell you that it is not my bag? My luggage is in the check room at Hamburg under this number and. . ."

"You will admit, will you not, that a person does not often leave his luggage behind in the check room at Hamburg when taking an express train to Paris? Well, well, we will telegraph!"

Six hours elapsed before Allan again saw the police magistrate with his round cheeks, mustache and spectacles. When he did, it was in a small and very quiet room in the immense Government building. The little man with his pedantic air was thumbing over a couple of telegrams, and kept looking first at a map of the German empire and then at an album containing many photographs.

"Well, well; we have investigated, we have telegraphed. . . I must admit, Mr. Kragh, you have had most extraordinary experiences. Is this your first extended trip abroad?"

"Yes," in an exasperated tone.

"That's what I thought. I can well imagine that. Most extraordinary experiences, I must say."

"Have you been able to establish my identity?" (In a decidedly exasperated tone; six hours' seclusion on Spartan fare does not tend to improve the temper.)

"We believe so. Yes, we believe we can feel convinced that you really are Mr. Allan Kragh of Sweden."

"You are thinking of releasing me, then? You are thinking of exposing the populace of Cologne to this risk? Has the Eau-de-Cologne been locked up? And the Cathedral guarded?"

"One moment, Mr. Kragh. We are very sorry about our mistake, very sorry, and we will gladly make whatever reparation we can. Of course you will immediately be set at liberty." The police magistrate's tone of voice was so soft and conciliatory that it almost sounded as though he were speaking Finnish. "Only, let me ask you one question: Was there anything of very great value in your luggage in Hamburg?"

"Of value? Hm. The usual articles a person takes with him on a trip, a few suits and things of that sort. No money or jewels."

"Well, that's good. . . The receipt they gave you at the check-room bore number 374?"

"Yes. What do you mean?"

"Just wait a moment! Hm. . . Three hundred and seventy-four. Well, Mr. Kragh, why should I conceal the fact from you? Your luggage has been stolen."

"Stolen? Do they steal luggage left at a railway check room in Germany? I have the receipt."

"Yes, yes, your receipt, No. 374, calling for three articles. But day before yesterday, when you—when you were arrested by mistake, a telegram was received at the check room to send immediately the three pieces on check No. 374 to Osnabrück; the owner had not found time to call for them. The people at the check room had them forwarded that afternoon; at six o'clock the same evening they were delivered up in Osnabrück (in return for a receipt which was counterfeit as we have every reason to believe, yes, every reason) to a gentleman who immediately continued on his journey to Holland. . . It seems, therefore, Mr. Kragh, that your trunk, your travelling-bag and overcoat have been stolen."

"Putz weg! Donnerwetter. . ." Allan stared at the mild-eyed police magistrate, while he gave vent to his feelings through these Germanisms. "Who in the name of Heaven. . ."

"Yes, who could have found out the number on the receipt for your luggage? Was someone spying on you in the station at Hamburg? We seem to understand the matter as little as you, yourself—and you *should* understand it better than we. Yes, you certainly should."

Allan burst into a new channel of thought.

"Yes, I certainly should! But how did you happen to arrest me? Why did you give that rascal the opportunity of stealing my luggage? Kindly explain what lies behind this other matter! I am now no longer under accusation!"

"Mr. Kragh!" The police magistrate's voice was full of mild reproach, but Allan no longer lent an ear to such pleadings; the thought of the injustice he had been made to suffer began to goad him on. Arrested like a criminal and then robbed into the bargain! It was too much. What do we have consuls for? He heard the police magistrate's mild-toned voice, as though seeing the world through rose-colored spectacles:

". . . that the whole affair originated in the restaurant-car. You did not know the person you dined with?"

"Know him? I never saw the fellow before in my life. This is the first time I have been abroad."

"Hm, yes, I can. . . Well, that person—but wait, you shall hear the story first hand."

The police magistrate pressed a button, gave orders to an attendant and while waiting for them to be carried out, began to turn over the leaves of the album containing the many photographs. Every few moments he raised his lower lip half up to his nose, apparently deeply pondering over some plan; now and then his ideas found expression through a thoughtful p-r-m, p-r-m, reminding one of the gurgling sound which issues from a toy trumpet after a small child has been blowing in it for a while. Suddenly the door opened and the attendant entered with someone who proved to be the restaurant-car waiter of the day before yesterday. The first thing he did made Allan think of those words of Börne: das deutsche Volk ist ein Lakaien-volk, for he had never in return for any tip seen so many and such humble bows as this serving-brother of his distributed to the right of him and to the left of him. The little police magistrate stopped the waiter with a gesture and said shortly:

"Tell your story. Explain the matter to this gentleman."

"Oh, sir, it is a mistake, a terrible mistake. He tricked me, he deceived me, gnädiger Herr. It was the gentleman who had dinner at your table—Teufel hol' ihn. Just as I was serving you with the fish, sir, the other gentleman screwed up his face and moved his lips so I could understand: 'Look at that gentleman there! He's wanted by the police!'—He was very careful so that you wouldn't notice, sir. I looked at you, sir, and heard you say something, sir, about having to travel without your luggage and everything; the other gentleman kept nodding and nodding at me—may the devil take him. Later he came out to where I was in the other part of the car and said, 'The gentleman at my table is none other than Mirzl himself.'"

"But who is Mirzl?" cried Allan, who now for the third time had this name slung at him. As answer the police magistrate silently handed him the album with the many pictures and a two-day-old Berlin newspaper. There, in a prominent place stood the headlines: '*Great Hotel Robbery in Berlin W. —Benjamin Mirzl again in action. Amount stolen over seventy thousand. Mirzl escapes in auto.*' In the album Allan found a series of photographs, full-face, profile and back view of a gentleman about thirty years old, whose features he seemed dimly to remember, probably from some illustrated weekly.

"Our biggest swindler," said the police magistrate. "He has never been caught; but this time he barely escaped and had to leave part of his loot behind him."

"That was the day before I left on the express!" cried Allan.

"Yes, that's when it was."

The serving-brother untiringly went on with his story.

"I naturally pricked up my ears; the other gentleman drew out his visiting card and said: 'I am Dr. Hauser, the lawyer.'"

"But he told me his name was Koch, and that he was an actor," cried Allan.

"He wished to mislead you, sir.—'I am Dr. Hauser, the lawyer,' he said to me. 'I am going to jump off at Essen so as to get hold of a detective and arrest Mirzl; if I don't get back in time, then, for the Lord's sake, see that he is arrested at Cologne! Police are always on hand at the station there. Remember that in connection with this last affair alone there is a reward of 5,000 marks!' That's what that cursed person said, and then jumped off the train at Essen. He didn't return, I kept an eye on you, sir, and in Cologne—"

"I know the rest," said Allan.

"Oh, sir, I am a poor man and married and have four children, and how could I know that this cursed person would bring about my ruin? He didn't even pay for his dinner before he jumped off the train at Essen."

"I won't pay for it. But I won't appear against you. I would advise you, however, to pay more attention to your serving another time and less to your customers. That is a good rule for a waiter, I believe."

"Oh, sir, I—"

"That's all right!" Then turning to the police magistrate, Allan said, "May I go now?"

"Why—why, of course. And you—you do not intend to bring an action for false arrest?"

"Not this time. I set out in search of adventure and if I get more than I bargained for I can't complain. In case my luggage should show up—but there is no sense in thinking about that. It was probably Mirzl who appropriated that too."

"P-r-m, oh, no! He goes in for higher class work than that!"

"Well, anyway, I am just as eager to become better acquainted with him as you are. Goodbye!"

Allan walked out of that small room in the big building; the little police magistrate accompanied him through the corridors and even as far as the door leading to the street. Here he and Allan, both bowing deeply, took final leave of each other. Allan, a bit befuddled from all that had happened, wandered through the streets without paying attention to the direction he took. It was almost four o'clock in the afternoon, he noticed. Suddenly, as he was standing on a street corner thinking over what he should do, he felt a hand on his shoulder and gave a start. Was he being arrested again? That would be too much of a good thing. He turned around. A young man in a straw hat smilingly greeted him and handed him a letter.

"For you," he said. Before Allan could stop him he was gone.

Allan stared after him in the crowd without knowing what to believe. He ran a few steps in the direction which the unknown had taken but without catching sight of him; the traffic at the moment was too dense. He then looked at the letter which was addressed to "Mr. Allan Kragh of Sweden," and tore it open, a sudden presentiment coming over him.

This is what he read:

My dear Mr. Kragh:

You have without doubt called down many a curse on my head since last we saw one another, although it is doubtful whether you really knew where to address your curses. Forgive me that I have so ill repaid your kindness in sharing with me your bottle of Graacher Auslese in the restaurant-car; forgive me still more, for the discomfort I later brought upon you—discomfort, the character of which I myself can imagine only too well.

I know that the loss of the few travelling effects left in Central Station at Hamburg, the check for which—No. 374—you imprudently showed me at dinner, is of little consequence compared to the other discomfort. However, I was really obliged, through force of circumstances, to act as I did, both in regard to the appropriation of your luggage and the other inconvenience caused you. You may be sure that it was indeed a case of absolute necessity.

Should you be disposed to let me try to atone for all the unpleasantness you have suffered and of course, above all, to allow me the opportunity of returning your sumptuous luggage, then you might meet me on Friday evening, the 12th of this month, at ten o'clock in the Leicester Lounge, Leicester Square, London. You may be sure I will

know you again, if you put in an appearance,
even though you may not recognize me. I propose
this in order to see whether I have rightly judged
the character of a man who, through a mere
whim, starts out on a journey and without more
ado leaves his luggage behind him.

And so, auf Wiedersehen!

Yours sincerely,

LUDWIG KOCH, alias Dr. Hauser, alias. . . (to
be filled in yourself as you see fit!)

P. S. I hope you will not take it amiss that I took
pains to inform myself of your name.

How many times Allan, standing in the midst of the crowd on Jülich Street, read this letter through it would be difficult to say. Finally the passers-by saw him pull himself together, stick the letter in his pocket, ask a policeman a question, and then hurry away in the direction of the railway station. It was after four o'clock; he had sufficient time to catch a certain train which he had just found out from the custodian of the law was due to leave within the hour, but during this time he must also satisfy the inner man after his trials and tribulations while under arrest.

"It's beginning!" murmured Mr. Kragh to himself. "What a fine sort of travelling companion I had! And that's how my luggage happened to disappear! Now, first of all, I will fulfil man's supreme and most inalienable right—

41

eating breakfast. It comes rather late but it is well earned. And then on to London to make the acquaintance of Mr. Benjamin Mirzl! It should be interesting."

CHAPTER II

THE BIG HOTEL

At one time Allan had paid a visit to the largest of those large turbine-engine plants in the south of Sweden. It seemed to him as though he were again among those engines, again in that oppressively throbbing and rumbling atmosphere, when late in the evening of the 11th of September he arrived in London.

He rubbed his eyes as he sat in the taxi-cab. This was a city! Here adventure must dwell; here it must be lying in wait just around the corner of every street. What were Hamburg and Cologne compared to this! What was that indescribable atmosphere of bustling haste, studied luxury, the fabulous expenditure of money which had been his impression of the train deluxe on his way north from Cologne, compared to London! Even the air was different, a mixture of a thousand ingredients, giving free rein to fancy in the odors arising from the hot pavements, in the smell of stale, scented Virginia tobacco, in the petrol vapors from countless numbers of automobiles, the rubber tires hissingly whishing over the smooth burnished asphalt; it was the perfume of all this world's fragrant riches and the stench of all its inexpressible poverty. Houses rushed by his automobile as though he were in a dream, the gigantic façades of the buildings disappearing far above in the hazy evening air; countless lights flamed and flickered; blazing advertisements crept up and down the buildings like rainbow-colored serpents; the sky hanging over the open squares burned an ashy red like the reflected glow from some tremendous conflagration or gigantic volcano in eruption. And the floods of humanity streamed on and on. The taxi-cab, bearing Allan Kragh of Sweden in search of adventure and—if luck would have it—a future, rushed noiselessly ahead through the confusing masses; avoiding collision, avoiding murder, momentarily cleaving at some street corner the floods of humanity; onward ever onward it rushed, apparently as meaninglessly as the thousand other motor cars it met, tenfold quicker than the forward rushing human stream but yet with just as little meaning. Suddenly it turned into an open square less brightly illuminated than the preceding streets and stopped in front of a façade where the lights were clustered together in a huge festoon. "Grand Hotel Hermitage" glowed this festoon of light; the chauffeur repeated it as he threw open the door of the taxi-cab and then Mr. Allan Kragh ascended a broad stairway into an immense hall which was unbelievably quiet and still after the Souza-march-symphony of the streets—the large revolving door to the vestibule clipping off the noise and clatter of the outer world as completely as would the portals to a convent.

This, then, was the renowned Grand Hotel Hermitage! A hundred times had Allan seen those three words in Henschel, in Bradshaw and the big flapping foreign newspapers and each time he had thought: only to be there! And now that he was adrift on his great voyage of chance and through Mr. Mirzl had been driven onward to London it was self-evident why he had given the chauffeur the address of this big hotel.

In Belgium, on his way from Cologne, Allan had provided himself with the most necessary travelling effects—one should not, perhaps, take Mr. Mirzl's promise too seriously, but on the other hand it would be stupid to burden one's self with double equipment. He was not entirely without luggage therefore, when, with a hotel attendant close at his heels, he entered through the revolving door; nevertheless it was only natural that the grave-mannered porter of the palatial hotel (whose figure most closely resembled a Benedictine bottle) should receive him in a somewhat condescending manner. Behind the porter Allan caught a glimpse in the office of a robust man, with grayish goatee—the manager of the hotel, as he was to learn later on. Had the manager and the porter been able to foresee the events which were to take place at the Grand Hotel Hermitage during Allan's visit there, and the rôle which Allan was destined to play, it is probable they would have greeted him in an entirely different manner than the way in which the porter received him.

"This is all the luggage you have, sir?"

"Yes; I am expecting more. I would like a room."

The porter looked him over a moment longer and then softer emotions seemed to gain the upper hand.

"A small room for this gentleman, Jones. Is 417 vacant?"

417 proved to be vacant. A thin young man in uniform took possession of Allan's meager luggage and conducted him to the elevator. This started on its way with the dignified leisure of an old family servant in some manor, and eventually came to a stop at the fourth floor. The gentleman in uniform led Allan the length of the carpeted corridor to the tiny room which was considered fit accommodation for him. It was really small, that is, in breadth, for the height left nothing to be desired; most of the space was taken up with a bed and dresser and on account of its architectural shape closely resembled a sepulchral chamber in some Egyptian pyramid. At the further end, Allan noticed, was a bathroom.

But Allan had learned from his university years that nothing is of less consequence than the room a person occupies during his travels as no-one ever remains there when awake or when sober; therefore he declared himself satisfied with the Egyptian sepulchre, pressed a shilling in the hand of the uniformed gentleman and started to clean up a bit.

When he, a half hour later, without any feeling of embarrassment at appearing in his travelling suit, strolled into the dining room of the big hotel, he had opportunity to realize that it is not only the rooms for those who travel with little luggage which are small; the world itself is extremely small. Yes, it was a most obvious fact, for when he had seated himself at a table, asked for the menu and had begun to look about him in the dining room—whom did he see sitting at the next table to his right, but the lady who, in the station at Hamburg, had lured him out into the world, and with her, as cavalier, the old gentleman with the hawk-like nose and the yellowish-gray mustache!

Allan stared at them in surprise. It was undeniably strange to meet just this pair here! Why, there were a thousand other hotels in London. Well, of course it was mere chance, but the bond of friendship which he had seen formed on the express train and to which he himself had been a contributing cause, was apparently of a more lasting kind than is usual with travelling acquaintanceship. He could well understand the reasons of old Bordeaux-nose, and in spite of the grudge which he still held against the young lady on account of her behavior in the railway carriage, he had to admit to himself that she was worthy of praise. . . she even seemed to him worthy of much praise. It would take the imagination of a Parisian, he thought, to plan such a costume as she wore that evening, and the courage of an American like her to wear it. His gaze wanderingly lost itself in the décolleté line around her soft bosom as coquettishly bared as though she were posing for a sketch by Rops, and as his eyes wandered over the white flesh and the green silk, it is possible they strayed down to where the tight skirt parted half-way up to her knee. . . what lines are more mystical and tempting to follow than those gracefully curving upward from a beautifully formed ankle? Especially when enclosed in a stocking of that discreet transparency of which Madame evidently approved. . . The rounding curves were outlined through the green silk like marble gleaming through the clear water of the Adriatic. Allan stared, fully aware that his manner was bold, when suddenly Madame turned her head (she had been sitting with her profile half turned in his direction) and let her gaze glide over him; Allan saw that he was recognized. At the same moment the waiter appeared at his table with the menu and wine-list, and he was compelled to remove his eyes from her.

Who could she be and how did it happen that she was here in such society? These questions buzzed around in Allan's head while he chose a couple of items from the menu and a Bordeaux from the wine-list. The waiter disappeared and he again had a clear view of the other table. They seemed to be carrying on a rather animated conversation. Was he the subject? It was not impossible, for her glance darted across to his table again for a fleeting second; the old gentleman with the hawk-like nose, however, showed no sign of interest in Allan, if they really were talking about him. Allan again began to look at her admiringly, seemingly without her paying any further attention to it, and he was still gazing when the waiter arrived with the omelet and the wine he had ordered. He took a sip from his glass and began to eat, his thoughts roving from the mysterious couple across the way to Mr. Benjamin Mirzl. Suddenly he recollected, and queerly enough for the first time, that it was just this trio—the old gentleman, the young lady and Mr. Mirzl—he had seen grouped together in front of the ticket-window at Hamburg. To be sure, they seemed to be entirely independent of each other then, but. . . Mr. Mirzl was an international swindler, even though perhaps of an eccentric and kindly sort; were the other two in the same class? Of course, this might be true and Allan kept thinking over the possibilities while he finished his chicken and Bordeaux and passed on to dessert with a glass of Madeira (a person must celebrate on arriving at the mother of all cities), but then he let the matter drop as improbable after his second glass of Madeira. He ordered coffee and liqueur, whereby the manner of the waiter began to be as mild and submissive as though Allan were in evening dress. He remained seated enjoying these pleasant beverages even after the pair who so mystified him had left the dining room. To his very great surprise, he noticed that she paid for both when the bill was presented; the old gentleman, therefore, must have been her guest. "A continental custom," thought Allan. They passed his table without sign of recognition or did he see aright when he thought he noticed a tiny twinkle, the mocking suggestion of a smile, in her eyes? It was impossible to determine.

At half-past ten, when Allan had decided on an evening's walk through London while smoking his cigar, he found that the city, in its turn, had decided to celebrate his arrival with an impenetrable yellowish-gray, smoky fog, with the result that (after two whiskies and soda in honor of the gigantic city) he retired to his Egyptian sepulchre. He immediately went to bed and slept like a log.

London is a wonderful city, full of surprises, inscrutable as the human heart, containing more things than Philosophy has ever dreamed about or Baedeker in his red books has ever starred; and Mr. Allan Kragh already found opportunity in his unassuming way to verify these *loci communes* during the following day. The fog of the evening before had been succeeded by a mild, humid sunshine, radiating from a mild, veronica-blue heaven, when in the forenoon he began his rambles from the Grand Hotel Hermitage, and obeying Goethe thrust himself into the crowding human life on the streets. His rambles, however, have nothing to do with this veracious narrative and we are content to join him again on his return to the Grand Hotel Hermitage about one o'clock that night. It was not the mysteries of London which then were bothering his brain; it was that mystery of a Benjamin Mirzl.

What had been Mr. Mirzl's idea with the letter which had been delivered to Allan by some accomplice two days before while in Cologne? A hoax? But why? Would a man of his sort amuse himself in that way? Of course, it was possible, but it did not fit in with the conception Allan had formed of Mr. Mirzl. It was also possible that this conception was as unlike the real Mr. Mirzl as Mr. Mirzl himself, when in disguise, was said to be unlike his own person. Be that as it may, on the stroke of nine, an hour before the appointed time, Allan had arrived at the café appointed by Mirzl, the Leicester Lounge. His impressions of London had thereby been increased by one; but when at half-past twelve (police closing hour) he had been driven from the café, this was the only benefit he had derived from his visit. As far as the café was concerned, his three-and-a-half-hour visit had proven of more benefit. The Leicester Lounge, it seemed, was a café of the kind where Mary Magdalene had access before her repentance. There were some two dozen Magdalenes in the café in front of the bar, and a half dozen behind. The rest of the very limited space was occupied by London's light-living masculinity. The watchword for this light-living masculinity of London, as well as for the management of the place, was 'prompt dispatch'. The greatest possible pleasure to the greatest possible number; a very worthy sentiment. The celerity of circulation was remarkable: *Entrée,* a drink, acquaintance, another drink, *sortie*. Gentlemen who made no acquaintances were eyed askance. Mr. Allan Kragh was eyed askance. It availed him nothing that he ordered a drink whenever the waiter's dark eyes met his, or that the glasses of an indefinite number of Magdalenes were filled at his table; he remained seated and accordingly was eyed askance. And Mr. Mirzl did not come. Or at least, he did not make himself known. Could it amuse him to be there in disguise, and watch Allan's bibulous waiting? Could he (there was the waiter eyeing him again—"Whiskey and soda, please!") could he have fallen into the hands of justice? The bulls in London kept a sharp look-out. Wasn't Mirzl cunning enough to trick them? Sherlock Holmes, you know. Anyway ("Whiskey and soda, please!" to the waiter eyeing him) —he was sufficiently clever to trick Allan Kragh. After three and a half hours of whiskey-orgy, Mr. Allan Kragh (on account of the police regulations and a feeling of weariness in his throat) left the Leicester Lounge, filled with the above mentioned convictions.

And the first things he saw in his Egyptian sepulchre No. 417 was his very own Swedish luggage. He was not far from believing that perhaps he had been indulging in a drop too much.

But it was a fact, both of the pieces were there; one of brown cow-hide, the other of iron-bound wood. . . His ringing at the bell brought a uniformed attendant to the grave chamber in less than a minute.

"This luggage?"

"Left here by a messenger at half-past nine this evening. There is a letter for you on the dresser, sir. Do you wish anything else, sir?"

Allan gave a slight wave of his hand. The whole affair seemed brimming over with mystery.

How in—how could Mr. Benjamin Mirzl have found out where he was living? Without bothering himself further over this amazing question he seized the letter on the dresser. It contained two keys and the following lines:

Dear Mr. Kragh:

Please forgive me for allowing you to wait in vain at the Leicester Lounge. Business, you know; it was impossible for me to come.

Hope you were not obliged to indulge in all too many whiskeys and soda; I know the place; sorry if you had to. I enclose the keys I used during the time I had your luxurious luggage in my possession; hope you can make use of them as duplicates; thanks once more for the loan of your luggage; again I beg your forgiveness for all the discomfort I have caused you, and remain in haste,

Yours sincerely,

LUDWIG KOCH, alias Dr. Hauser, alias. . . (to be filled in as you see fit).

It is unnecessary to record the exclamations, questions and gestures with which Allan Kragh commented on this epistle. "Life is short," as Mark Twain said. It was well past three o'clock before he lay down after going through his luggage for the third time—he found nothing missing—and after reading through Benjamin Mirzl's letter for the ninety-eighth time. It was an hour later before he dropped asleep and when he did his slumber was restless.

He really would be glad to meet Mr. Mirzl. It was ordained that his desires should be gratified in this respect, but there was still to be a slight delay.

* * *

It was late when Allan opened his eyes the next day. His first glance was toward his luggage and his second toward Mr. Mirzl's letter which he now knew by heart as though it was a Bible quotation in the catechism; not until the third glance did his eyes rest on the clock. It was five minutes of twelve. Allan jumped out of bed and began to dress. Just before falling asleep he had happened to think that there might be a chance of tracing Mr. Mirzl through the messenger who had brought the luggage. Allan knit his brows and laid out in his mind a plan of war based on the above-mentioned messenger, through which Mr. Mirzl would soon find himself discovered in his den.

But alas! the first threads quickly snapped when at half-past twelve he began making inquiries at the hotel office. The messenger? An ordinary messenger boy. His number? Lord knows what his number was. He simply had put down the bags, declared they were for the gentleman in 417 whose name was on the accompanying letter, and that everything was paid; whereupon he left without further remarks. Now, come to think of it, he didn't have a number. Most likely he was somebody out of work. Was anything wrong about the bags? Had the fellow stolen anything, or carelessly lost anything?

Allan hastened to tell him no and then quickly went away. Such matters were not so easy to discuss with an unromantic hotel employee. He tried to think out what Sherlock Holmes would have done in his place and suddenly an idea occurred to him. An advertisement! That was it. Sherlock Holmes would have inserted an advertisement in the paper offering a reward to the messenger without a number.

Allan inquired where the hotel news-stand was and found it situated in a small hall to the right of the main entrance. It was an extensive affair where they sold newspapers from all over the world, received advertisements and subscriptions to them, and where (in return for a slight fee) they accepted from the persons concerned notices for the papers about their stay at the Grand Hotel Hermitage, about their habits and their favorite sports. Allan was given a blank form and after a little thought formulated the following advertisement:

> *Messengers. Two pounds reward will be paid the messenger who on the evening of the 12th at half-past nine delivered three pieces of luggage at the Grand Hotel Hermitage, if he presents himself without delay at the said hotel.*

The clerk at the news-stand was a serious looking young man of the detective type; he took Allan's advertisement without any further comment than to ask Allan in which newspapers he wished it to appear. Allan left the decision to his judgment, whereupon the rather thin young man decreed that the *Star*, the *Daily Mail* and the *Daily Citizen* were the best and received a certain amount for two insertions of the advertisement in each of them. Well satisfied with himself, Allan went out to lunch.

In the course of the afternoon while walking along Pall Mall an idea struck him, however, which resulted in his springing from an auto in front of the Grand Hotel Hermitage fifteen minutes later. He had completely neglected to find out who was his mysterious travelling-companion, the lady from Hamburg! And they were both stopping at the same hotel! That's the way it goes when a person has his head full of just one thing. The porter with the figure of a Benedictine bottle was himself in charge of the hotel office when Allan entered for the purpose of starting his investigation. The porter's tone had grown several degrees warmer through the arrival of Allan's luggage.

"Do you wish a larger room, sir?" he asked.

"Perhaps later," said Allan. "At present there is something I should like to ask you about, porter."

For a moment he called to aid his recollections of Sherlock Holmes. "I think I have recognized an acquaintance here in the hotel, a lady. I am not absolutely sure and do not want to seem obtrusive, you can well understand, porter. She is blonde, slender, of medium height or a trifle over, makes a very good but trifle haughty appearance, and had dinner here in the dining room day before yesterday—"

He gave a sudden start as he heard the rustle of silk skirts at his side. He turned his head and there stood the fair unknown herself.

"I happened to hear your friendly inquiries," she said. "Surely it can't be I whom you are describing to the porter?"

This time there could be no doubt, as there had been

a couple of days before in the dining room, about the expression on her face. Now it was exactly the same glance which he remembered from the express train, a look in the gray eyes that chilled him to the marrow. At last he pulled himself together.

"You, Madame? As far as I know, I have not the pleasure of knowing you."

"Nor I you—by name."

There was a withering inflection on the last two words which expressed only too well what she meant—the scene in Cologne where, five days before, she had seen him arrested. Allan turned a beautiful red, but managed to say: "Without doubt you wish to speak to the porter. I will withdraw so there can be no question of eavesdropping on my part."

He knew that this parting thrust must strike deep down in her Anglo-Saxon heart, but in spite of that fact he felt his departure from the office could not be called a *sortie d'eclat*. He cut across the vast lobby as quickly as his dignity would allow—fearing most of all that she would call him back and request him to continue his questioning of the porter, a task which at the moment he did not feel able to face; then without realizing where his legs had been taking him, he suddenly found himself standing in the lounging-room of the hotel and heard a voice in his immediate vicinity hurl forth an unusually vehement "Hell and damnation." Not until a moment later did it dawn on him that it was he himself who had uttered the words, and while still surprised at his quick progress in becoming anglicized, he heard someone say in a shrill voice:

"Hello, young man! Such expressions are not used in the presence of ladies."

Allan turned around. In spite of being at the moment in anything but an amicable frame of mind toward his fellow men, he had to smile.

In one of the red leather easy chairs sat an old lady holding a *New York Herald* in her hand—she would have been hidden behind the newspaper if she had not lowered it just then and peeked at Allan over the top. Her face looked exactly like that of an old, shrewd parrot; she had gray hair which stood out around her ears, two keen, coal-black eyes and a nose which dominated the rest of her face as completely as St. Paul's does the open square on which it stands. Like the cathedral, it did not attain its full architectural effect through lack of perspective. . . One saw, however, a wide mouth with thin and very severe looking lips and a chin which did its best to produce a Napoleonic effect. The coal-black eyes were fixed on Allan with a sidelong glance, exactly as though they were those of a parrot. They seemed indescribably shrewd and stern. Allan bowed respectfully:

"I beg your pardon a thousand times, Madame! I really wasn't thinking of what I did, and hardly realized where I was."

"Why did you swear?" asked the old lady. She placed an intonation on the word 'swear' so that it sounded like 'murder' or 'bear false witness.'

Allan was seized with an absurd impulse to tell her the

whole story.

"I will try to explain," he began. "Are you an American, if I may ask?"

"Yes. Do you consider that an excuse for your swearing?"

"Not because *you* are an American, Lord forbid. But to tell the truth it was one of your countrywomen who was the cause of my swearing."

"A gentleman never swears about a lady, nor in the presence of ladies."

"You are absolutely right. I am sorry from the bottom of my heart. You see, this lady caught me unawares just as I was in the act of questioning the porter. . ."

"Had she been listening? Then she can't be called a lady. Then you had a perfect right to swear."

"Hm, you see, I was asking the porter about her. . ."

"Are you in love with her? Then you had a right to ask him. Then I can understand your actions."

"She interested me. And you understand, that. . ."

"Did you find out from the porter who she is? Are you English?"

"She came just in the nick of time to prevent me. No, I am Swedish, Madame."

"Then why did you swear in English?"

"Who knows? The climate, perhaps. Once more I beg your pardon, Madame."

"Oh, demmit, don't bother about that. I swear, too, when it is necessary. Sit down, you interest me. What are you doing in London?"

"If I only knew. Strictly speaking, I am here to meet a gentleman who stole my luggage."

"You'll never get it back. In London you never get anything back, not even the change that you are supposed to receive after paying a bill. I know these Englishmen. Did he steal your luggage here in London?"

"No, on an express-train in Germany; and, you see, the ridiculous part. . ."

"What is the ridiculous part? There is Helen. Hello, my dear! What is the ridiculous part?"

"That he sent all my things back unharmed."

"Now, demmit—I mean, what are you doing, sitting there and making fun of me, young man? Helen, come here and you will hear something worthwhile. Here is a young man who tells stories like those from the Thousand and One Nights. In addition, he swears in the presence of ladies."

Allan looked up and saw a young girl of twenty, who now came toward the old lady in the easy chair. She was willowy, blonde, and undeniably an American. Allan had an instinctive feeling of sympathy for her, a sympathy which he just as instinctively realized was different to the feelings he usually cherished toward young ladies. She had gray eyes and very clear-cut features. If she was the daughter of the old lady in the easy chair, then she must more closely favor her father.

"This is my daughter, young man, even if you can't believe it."

The coal-black parrot-like eyes had evidently read his thoughts. Allan bowed and drew out a visiting card.

"I do not know what is customary in America," said he, a trifle embarrassed. "May I?"

The old lady grasped his card with claw-like fingers, held it warily at arm's-length (in this case not such a very great distance) and read it with head bent to one side.

"K-r-a-g-h! Kragh! What a funny name! Well, my name is Mrs. Bowlby, of Worcester, Massachusetts, sir!"

She pronounced Allan's name as if it were spelled Cray. Allan tried to bring about a pronunciation nearer to the Scandinavian.

"Now, demmit, do you think I came to England to learn Swedish? If you can make use of an English oath you can also make use of an English name. There, go on with your story."

Consequently, while in Mrs. Bowlby's company it was as Mr. Cray that Allan passed through his further experiences.

Under a torrent of questions, he related his adventures on the German express train, in Cologne, and in London. Suddenly the old lady's thoughts dashed back to the starting point.

"And the lady whom you saw in the station at Hamburg is the same one who is stopping here at the hotel?"

"Yes."

"How can the hotel permit such a thing? Of course she is an adventuress. Even the way she behaved to a well-bred young man like you proves it."

"Mrs. Bowlby, I was very bold. . ."

"Certainly not. Absolutely not. She is an adventuress, mark my words. What does she look like?"

"She is a trifle over medium height and somewhat haughty; has gray eyes like Miss Bowlby and a short upper lip. She looks like a blonde Spanish Infanta, if you understand what I mean Mrs. Bowlby."

"Of course. And she is an American?"

"Yes. At least I believe so. That is to say, in the station she spoke German fluently, as I have already told you, although later on. . ."

"Ha! ha!" Mrs. Bowlby's laugh was like the harsh triumphant cry of a parrot which had just succeeded in taking a good nip out of the forefinger of some enemy:

"German! I have seen her in the hotel, you may be sure of that! Now I know whom you mean. She could have spoken French just as well, young man. Fine company you have fallen into! Do you think I don't know who she is? Mrs. Langtrey, do you remember Mrs. Langtrey, Helen?"

"You have spoken of her, I am sure, Mamma."

"I? Never, as long as I've lived. I don't speak of such persons. Someone else, perhaps, may have told you about her—four years ago everyone was talking about her although they should be ashamed to mention such matters."

"Why, Mamma!"

"Hush! I know what I am saying. Dash it, I shouldn't speak of her to you, Helen! She was married to Captain

Langtrey in Boston and way up in society. Just before Langtrey died, she had an outrageous flirtation with some Frenchman, who called himself baron or marquis or king. De Citrac was his name. Langtrey's eyes were scarcely closed when she disappeared. Went to Europe. Of course, everyone knew why she went there. Since then no one in America has heard of her, although everyone has been talking about her. But yesterday when we came I thought I saw her here in the hotel, and now after Mr. Cray's description. . ."

Mrs. Bowlby's oration was interrupted through the door to the lounging-room being opened and in came somebody in a bright rose-colored dress which swished about her like spray around a slender column. She cast a look of icy indifference at Allan without so much as a glance at the two ladies, and with queenly grace went over to one of the tables where the illustrated weeklies lay. She choose a copy of *The Queen*, and settled down out of hearing distance in one of the leather chairs at the further end of the lounging-room.

"Well!" Mrs. Bowlby's interjection contained a world of meaning. "If that isn't she, the. . ."

Allan, who had been staring in the same direction as had Mrs. Bowlby with those coal-black eyes of hers, at last slowly withdrew his gaze. Noticing his glance, Mrs. Bowlby arose from her chair and stood before him full five feet high.

"Tea-time," she said. "Will you join Helen and me at tea, Mr. Cray? You need shelter and protection from the world, young man. It is full of sin, and our flesh is Sin's best ally."

Allan opened the door for her and Miss Helen while inwardly he regretted, partly that Sin could appear so attractive, and partly that it was not always so willing to attack people as the theologians claim.

* * *

At tea in Mrs. Bowlby's sitting room on the first floor he met Mr. Bowlby, a tall, broad-shouldered, light-haired man, apparently younger than his wife. His smooth-shaven face received its mark of character from the large cheerful mouth. He looked like an overgrown schoolboy. Mrs. Bowlby introduced Allan by the name under which she had once and for all decided his identity should be hidden. She gave a vivid description of his adventures and a still more highly-colored account of Mrs. Langtrey and her opinions of what this lady amounted to. Mr. Bowlby punctuated her story with many a "blow me!" and cup of tea. Finally he wiped his mouth and said:

"Well, Susan," (his voice was loud and gruff like that of a large overgrown puppy), "I have some news, too. We must move up to the second floor."

"You'll see me hanged first," said Mrs. Bowlby without hesitation. "Has the stock market gone back on you, John? You should leave it alone when you are away on a vacation."

"It isn't the market," said John. "It is a king."

"A king? Have you been lending money to a king, John?"

"Nonsense, I don't lend money, you know that. The king is going to stop here, a real king, and he's coming day after to-morrow so as to get married here in London. The manager asked me, just as a favor, to. . ."

"There's one thing I want to say, John. Don't try to marry off our poor child to him! Helen, you must never think about men of that sort, promise me that, my child."

"You're raving, Susan. Let Helen marry him! I would as willingly give her to a Mormon bishop. The king who is coming here already has a hundred and fifty wives."

"Lord have mercy on us! What sort of a monster is it who wants to drive us out of our apartment, John?"

"A king, a real king with fifteen million subjects, brown the most of them, but blow it, a real king. The manager was absolutely in despair because. . ."

"Don't talk to me about the manager! Aren't you a free-born American citizen? Aren't there other hotels in London?"

"A few, Susan, but this is certainly the only one where a king can stop. And we are to be given an apartment one flight higher up, the one where Prince Hieronymus of Bulgaria lived when last in London."

"Then this king can just as well be satisfied with that, too. What is good enough for one is good enough for the other."

"This one here is a reigning prince, Susan, and a reigning prince can't live higher up than the first floor."

Mrs. Bowlby's coal-black eyes wandered from John to Miss Helen and from her to Allan.

"Has he got his hundred and fifty wives with him, John?"

"That I don't know, Susan dear. If so, he'll probably hire

a special hotel for them. Or perhaps a hundred and fifty, so they won't make life too uncomfortable for him."

Mrs. Bowlby relented.

"I am sure he has them with him, John, I know men. Well, we'll move up to the prince's apartment. I must stay here and protect this young man. It is my duty, Mr. Cray, for I know women, too."

Mrs. Bowlby put her tea-cup down with an energetic manner, and looked at Allan as though he were a young parrot on the point of trying his wings for the first time. Then she turned to Mr. Bowlby.

"What's the Monster's name, John?"

"Yussuf Khan," answered Mr. Bowlby, lighting a cigar. "Yussuf Khan, Maharajah of Nasirabad."

CHAPTER III

Yussuf Khan, Maharajah
of Nasirabad

When Ibrahim Khan, autocratic Maharajah of
Nasirabad, a state in the north-western corner of
India, was defeated in 1885 at Khawak Pass by Sir George
Merriman, at that time Colonel in the Anglo-Indian
army, it was not a prince or a people that fell; it was a
system. Ibrahim Khan, during the forty years of his reign,
had made himself felt as the most bitter opponent to the
English rule since the time of Tippo Sahib; it was only the
smallness of his state and its out-of-the-way position which
had prevented his enmity from being as formidable as it
was bitter. When the news of the outcome of the battle
at Khawak Pass reached Nasirabad, and when it became
clear that the days of Ibrahim Khan's autocratic rule were
numbered, he decided that he himself should at least
determine the number of those days. He chose to throw
himself on his sword, and the smoke, which Sir George at
the time of his entry saw ascending over the flat roofs of

Nasirabad, arose from Ibrahim's Khan's funeral pyre and not from a bonfire of joyous welcome.

However, it is well known (we draw the reader's attention to the excellent biography of Sir George Merriman by Alexander Carton, Heinemann & Co., London, 1908) that Ibrahim Khan's conqueror was passed master in the art which Hannibal never learned—that of reaping the benefit of his victory. Appointed administrator of the kingdom he had won for the Queen, he directed its affairs with a loyalty and zeal which even in India has probably seldom found a counterpart; but this was not all: he was rewarded with a success which in all likelihood has been attained still less frequently. When, in 1905 on the day of the anniversary of the battle at Khawak Pass, he left the deep valleys of Nasirabad, it was as the country's father, not its conqueror; genuine tears of sorrow from all classes of people accompanied his departure; and these tears were redoubled when the news of his death three months later reached this simple mountain folk. "He smote us; he became our father; and when that heart of his no longer heard the answering throbs of ours, then did his forever cease to beat," sang the old court poet, Abdul Mahbub.

The grief at Sir George's death was somewhat alleviated through a son of the old royal house, under the supervision of the new resident, Sir Herbert Layson, taking over at that time the reins of government. This was Yussuf Khan, Ibrahim Khan's eldest living son—himself one of the products, and perhaps not the most successful, of Sir

George Merriman's reforms. Only four years old at the time of Sir George's entry into Nasirabad, the young prince had immediately been placed under the charge of an English tutor; it was Sir George's belief that reforms like culture should begin from the top and work down. As tutor for the young Prince Yussuf, he selected an old Oxford friend named Bowles. Evidently Sir George chose him more on account of his friendship than for his ability as a pedagogue; it is also possible that he was too occupied with the other inhabitants of Nasirabad and their various affairs to have much time left over for the royal household with its many relatives. However that may be, the glory which surrounded the conqueror of Nasirabad tended to restrain any excesses on the part of the young heir to the throne, at least as long as Sir George himself had the reins of government in his hands. But the year 1906—Yussuf Khan's twenty-fifth year—was scarcely underway before he began to give Sir Herbert Layson something to think about.

By this time his old tutor Bowles was already out of the game, packed off to England with a good pension and with all the orders of the state of Nasirabad pinned upon his breast. His work had at least one effect: Yussuf Khan had learned to love the English language and hardly ever spoke his mother tongue, even to his suite. It was Sir Herbert himself who bore the brunt of the young regent's first attack against the new régime. He met the difficulty in his own peculiar way and perhaps that which now happened might never have occurred had a man of another character occupied Sir Herbert's position, in which case this book would never have seen the light of day. *Habent sua fata libelli*, rightly says the Roman poet. Now Sir Herbert Layson was a disciple of this very Roman poet and of Herbert Spencer, his great namesake; he was a sedate, ironic, industrious and reserved man, who attended to his day's work and amused himself by looking down, as though from a clear, cool height, on the life below, just as from his palace in Nasirabad, he looked down upon the deep valleys below the capital. Yussuf Khan's impetuosities of youth he caught, like javelins, upon his shield of irony; it must be admitted that the shield was severely put to test. It began with questions of administration in which the young regent wished to force through his own ideas; attacks in this quarter were of short duration. Sir Herbert let the young man have his own way in one or two appropriate cases; that was enough. The disturbances and commotions among the people, who were already accustomed to the English resident's rational ordinances and taxes, hastily convinced even Yussuf Khan that his talents lay more in other directions. And quickly enough he discovered what these directions were; namely, horse-racing and military sports. The attack lasted some two years or more, from 1907 until the end of 1909. Thereupon followed a short period of lassitude for the patient, before further symptoms of his malady put in an appearance. And when they began to show, Sir Herbert for the first time became uneasy. It was woman who made her entry into Yussuf Khan's life, and, what was worse, the

Dream Woman, the ideal woman seen only with the eyes of fancy. Sir Herbert had good grounds for uneasiness.

At this point the superficial reader may ask in surprise: Well, and what then? Have we not read about these Indian princes and their harems, where the most beautiful, the most alluring women in the world are carefully guarded for their masters, like a library of so many deluxe volumes? Are not their almond-shaped eyes darker and milder than those of a gazelle, are not their limbs more lithesome and pliant than entwining vines, their tender affection more seductive than hashish? Are there not zenana missions to help these unfortunates? Or was Yussuf Khan less fortunate than other Indian princes? To those readers who ask these elegantly formulated questions, we can only answer: Think of yourself in Yussuf Khan's position as sovereign lord and husband of a hundred and fifty beautiful women from Asia's many nations! What avails a harem and its arabesque embellished walls against an ideal? An ideal can always find some crack in the arabesque through which to force a way; it can simulate the tones of the nightingale, singing about women a thousand times more seductive than the Queen of the harem; it whispers through the murmuring palms; it rings like the song of a siren through the fountains. Or to express oneself as prosaically as did His Most Christian Majesty Francis I of France, also lord over a (of course highly Christian) harem—"tourjours perdrix!" Always partridges—live on partridges and Bordeaux for a month, and you will long for bread and cheese and a drink of water.

Live on partridges for a couple of years, and you will turn vegetarian. Yussuf Khan, Maharajah of Nasirabad, had definitely been converted to vegetarianism as early as the middle of 1909, and at the end of that year his idealistic sickness passed into an extremely acute state.

He wanted to marry a European princess!

Had Sir Herbert Layson cause to be uneasy, or not?

What made matters worse was the good Sir Herbert's own character. His skull absolutely lacked the bumps of ideality which a phrenologist would have found in Yussuf Khan; when Yussuf Khan for a while began to seek his companionship and hesitatingly sought to acquaint him with the tortures his soul was silently suffering, Sir Herbert met his confessions with a dry smile lurking behind his bushy mustache and with reflections on the women of Europe which made Yussuf Khan resentfully flare up like another Bayard. Not until it was too late did Sir Herbert realize how matters stood and changed his tactics; but no longer did his attempts at interesting the young Regent in polo or in questions of government meet with success. His only hope was that spring, which rekindles love among men, would also have its effect on Yussuf Khan. Spring came, and instead of rekindling the love for his hundred and fifty wives, Yussuf Khan's idealism burst into flames like watch-fires along the highways far up in the mountains. Furthermore, spring brought him a plan. As it was unlikely that the European princesses would seek him out in Nasirabad, there evidently remained nothing for him to do but search for them in Europe!

Now a real inferno began for Sir Herbert. Endless exhortations and ironical outbursts proved equally ineffective. Throughout the summer Yussuf Khan wandered around his palace like an unappeased spirit with but a single request on its lips. The summer at Nasirabad, otherwise cool and comfortable compared to the same season in other parts of India, slowly became hotter to Sir Herbert than Bikanir at its worst. His floods of irony dried up under the glowing heat of Yussuf Khan's Asiatic persistency. He became nervous and irritable, and lost both his cool calm way of looking at life's phenonema and his joy in work. At last toward the end of July he made up his mind and wrote to the Viceroy at Simla. Could one risk letting loose on Europe a Himalayan lion suffering with the feverish poison of idealism? Were the European princesses of marriageable age insured against such a calamity? Had Pasteur found no method of treatment for this new form of rabies?

The Viceroy's answer, which was awaited with unexampled suspense in Nasirabad, was short and to the point: "Let the young idiot go, but take care he is well watched."

Sir Herbert gave a sigh of infinite relief. Within a week the work on Yussuf Khan's equipment was in full sway—this length of time had been needed to modify the young Regent's ideas of the magnificence which should be displayed in the wooing of white princesses. After elephants, mares bedecked with cloth of gold caparisons, and an escort of two hundred dumb slaves had been struck from the program, there remained one point where he proved to be adamant: the crown jewels of Nasirabad, each and every one, should be taken along. Even with this magnificence he knew only too well how extremely small were his chances of approaching the proud princess of his dreams: without the jewels his prospects would be as infinitesimally small as the eggs of the white ant. Sir Herbert shrugged his shoulders; as a matter of fact, he could do nothing in this case since the jewels were Yussuf Khan's private property. He contented himself by having the jewels brought before him; it was a sight worth seeing. From hearsay, he knew about the jewels which Ibrahim Khan had stored away in his treasure house, but up to now they had been as carefully hidden from his eyes as the hundred and fifty ladies in Yussuf Khan's harem. It was a pyramid of diamonds, pearls, topazes, emeralds, rubies and gold, a waterfall of color sparkling with light. Half dazzled by what he had seen, he hastened to make arrangements for packing the treasures as carefully and securely as possible.

We will have occasion to mention them later.

On the fifteenth of August at break of day, Yussuf Khan with his train of followers left Nasirabad on his matrimonial quest. The sun was just rising behind the ridge of the Himalayas and the castle at Nasirabad with its slender towers lay as though snared in a net of white light. Cannons on the bastions thundered out their message of the Regent's departure and the people swarmed along the streets to see Yussuf Khan on his white horse ride out through the city gates where Sir George Merriman, twenty-five years before, had entered. Sir Herbert followed the Maharajah until the evening's first relay; then he turned back to his daily work happy in the consciousness that his difficult charge had been entrusted to the care of his old brusque friend, Colonel Morrel, military commander at Nasirabad for the past ten years; otherwise there was no person of rank in the suite excepting Yussuf Khan's aged native teacher, the sixty-year-old court poet, Ali.

The western sky between the walls of the valley, where Yussuf Khan and his retinue disappeared, shone like a strip of June roses, flaming red, above the dazzling mountain tops, white as the lilies of Easter—it was as though the heavens themselves were trying to herald aloud his wooing quest to the land of the white princesses. With a smile at the prospect of Yussuf Khan achieving his matrimonial plans, Sir Herbert turned his horse's head toward Nasirabad, glad that he could again in peace take up his work and again continue his ironical survey of life's phenomena from the Residence windows which looked out over the deep valleys of Nasirabad.

CHAPTER IV

THE BIG HOTEL
(CONTINUED)

"Were you up in time to see him, Miss Helen?"

"Of course. Not everybody stays in bed until lunch like you, Mr. Cray. That's a very pretty tie you are wearing."

"I am glad you like it. But how did he look?"

"Magnificent! He had on white tennis trousers and a silk hat."

"That wasn't much for September."

"Don't try to be witty. Of course he had on a number of other things, too. On the whole, he is rather good-looking, although inclined to be a little stout."

"How old is he?"

"He seemed to be about thirty or so. He has a black mustache and really fine-looking teeth. And the people with him—you should be ashamed of yourself for staying in bed so late!"

"Did he have elephants, camels and negroes with him?"

"At least there were negroes. There was but one white

man among them all, an old, gruff gentleman with a white mustache. The porter said he was an English Colonel who is to keep watch over the Monster, as Mamma calls him."

"And the rest were negroes?"

"If you want to call them so. They were dark-skinned, of course, but you may be sure they were a stately looking lot. He had a sort of body-guard of ten men with turbans and scimitars, who are to keep watch at his door day and night. And then there was an old gentleman, some sort of dignitary, I imagine, who was dressed in civilian clothes and looked as sanctimonious as an archbishop. He had a gray beard which was combed out on both sides, just like the advertisements you see in the newspapers."

"Those of the Hungarian pomade?"

"Exactly. Just before they started marching upstairs he read something in verse. It sounded like a bit of sorcery. I was really quite inspired."

"Did any genii appear? Didn't he rub a copper lamp, too?"

"That I can't say. He wore such wide clothes that I couldn't tell."

"Were they Eastern clothes?"

"At least they didn't come from New York. But anyway, he was a stately old gentleman. He looked a bit wild, and yet refined, if you know what I mean. Here comes Mamma."

Mrs. Bowlby, in white morning toilette, came skipping across the hall of the Grand Hotel Hermitage; both her feet seemed to move forward simultaneously like a bird hopping alone. A sharp chirp of satisfaction was heard as she caught sight of her daughter and Allan sitting in two of the large leather chairs. Allan hastened to draw up another, and Mrs. Bowlby disappeared in its depths like a lump of sugar in a cup of coffee.

"Thank goodness! I was beginning to think the Monster had already run away with you, Helen."

"Why, Mamma! He has a hundred and fifty sulta-nas now!"

"Oh, I know men. Whether they have a hundred and fifty or one, they are in either case deceivers."

"I can assure you he didn't even look at me."

"What did he look like, Helen?"

"He was really good-looking, although a trifle fat."

"With a hundred and fifty wives!"

"He was a bit eccentrically dressed, of course. But you should have seen his body-guard. Ten—but here is Papa. He looks as though he had something to tell us."

Mr. Bowlby came briskly toward them from across the hall, his face beaming with news.

"Good morning, everybody," he cried. "Well!"

"Now John, what is it?"

"Just keep quiet, Susan, and you shall hear all about it, although the matter must be kept as secret as possible on account of the thieves here in London."

"What is it, John? Is it about the hundred and fifty?"

"Not about the ones you mean. He has a hundred and fifty other trifles with him. . ."

"Three hundred in all!"

". . .which he considers of much more value. By Jove! The manager trembled in his very shoes. Their equal cannot be found in Europe and hardly in India."

"What are you talking about, Papa?"

"His jewels, my dear. A hundred and fifty pieces of jewelry and a lot of loose stones, all of a quality beyond compare. Colonel Morrel, the old Englishman who has come along to sort of look out for him, spoke of them, said the manager, as the eighth wonder of the world, although he otherwise does not strike one as being a person easily impressed by anything."

"Of course he has had them put in the hotel vault for safe-keeping, Mr. Bowlby?"

"No, my young friend, and that is just where the trouble comes. The Colonel insisted they should be handed over. But the Maharajah is determined to keep them in his apartment. Perhaps you can understand how nervous the hotel manager is! Just think if some rat of a hotel thief. . ."

"No rat of that kind gets into the Grand Hotel Hermitage, Mr. Bowlby! Besides, isn't the species extinct like the Plesiosaurus and the Pterodactyl?"

"Don't be so sure about that, Mr. Cray. I remember two years ago in New York—but that doesn't matter. Of course, he has his body-guard keeping watch outside his suite. . ."

"Our suite, John."

". . . day and night. You saw those ten wild-looking fellows with scimitars, Helen. They should be protection enough. But the manager mentioned something else, too."

"What, Papa? Was it about the gray-bearded bishop?"

"Bishop? That is his court poet and teacher: Ali is his name, I think. Did you hear him declaiming as he went up the steps, Helen? No, it was about the Maharajah himself. He is more eccentric than Pierpont Morgan, although in another way. J. Pierpont collects old things, because anything old is the only thing new he can hit upon. The Maharajah, who has *his* little house full of old things, has become tired of them, and do you know what he intends to do? To change the settings of all his jewels! He is afraid that otherwise the Europeans will hold him up to ridicule. *Well!*"

Mr. Bowlby's interjection came straight from the heart. He began looking around the hall when he suddenly stopped and let out another cry.

"Blow me! When one speaks of the devil. . . There is the man now, who has been called in to make the changes. The Maharajah is in a hurry! He has hardly had time to eat breakfast yet."

"Which one is he, Papa?"

"That man over there. The one with the big mustache, standing there talking to the hotel manager."

"By Jove!"

It was now Allan who gave vent to his feelings through this Anglo-Saxon method of expressing surprise. Just at the entrance to the hotel office, talking to the broad-shouldered man with the goatee, whom he knew to be the manager of the hotel, stood no less a person than his old acquaintance from the Central Station at Hamburg—the man with the Bordeaux-tinged, hawk-like nose and the bushy yellowish-gray mustache. The manager was talking to him in a most respectful manner and seemed to be giving him some sort of explanation. He kept shrugging his shoulders as though discussing something, the responsibility of which he did not wish to assume.

"What is the matter, Mr. Cray?"

Allan finally stopped looking at the two men. He waited a moment and then said in his most dramatic tone:

"What the matter is, Mrs. Bowlby? Nothing less than the fact that I know the man Mr. Bowlby was speaking about."

"You know him? What is his name?"

"Well. . . that I don't know."

"But I know," said Mr. Bowlby. "He is a Dutchman and his name is van Schleeten. He is one of the greatest jewelers or at any rate, jewel-specialists in Europe. It was he who made the magnificent diadem which the French Republic sent to the Empress of Russia and he has carried out scores of similar commissions. The manager told me all about it. He also confided to me that the good Mynheer van Schleeten has been a great Don Juan in his day. How do you happen to know him, Mr. Cray, without knowing who he is?"

"That is a specialty with Mr. Cray, John! He knew Mrs. Langtrey, too, without knowing her name."

Allan nodded.

"You are right, Mrs. Bowlby, and the remarkable thing is that I happened to meet them both at the same time. I travelled with them from Hamburg, you know, the time I had my luggage stolen. They were together."

"Then the jeweler is a swindler. Langtrey's wife knows no one but swindlers. He is planning to steal the Monster's jewels."

"Susan, you should be more careful how you speak about people. I have already told you who he is. Do you think the manager would dare to let a suspicious person slip by him, and get anywhere near the Maharajah's jewels, which, if your ideas are correct, he evidently intends to do now?"

Mrs. Bowlby only answered with a scornful toss of her head. She stared at the Bordeaux-nosed jeweler with a piercing look as he, with the manager at his side, quickly crossed the hall to the lift. Her nose silently but eloquently expressed the opinion she had formed of Mr. van Schleeten from what Allan had mentioned about his acquaintance with a certain lady. The manager and the Dutchman disappeared in the lift and Mrs. Bowlby jumped out of her chair like a Jack-in-the-box.

"Time for lunch," she declared. "Keep us company, Mr. Cray, and tell us how Langtrey's wife behaved to the jeweler."

The same day had a further surprise in store for Allan, and it came through a person whom he had almost forgotten since he had been spending his time with the Bowlby family, namely, Mr. Benjamin Mirzl.

The surprise again came in the form of a letter. Allan had just finished his after-dinner cigar in the smoking-room when one of the innumerable attendants of the hotel came in and quickly looking around the room, steered his course straight towards Allan.

"A letter for you, sir."

Allan looked up, somewhat surprised. Who could be writing letters to him here?

"For me?"

"For you, sir. Aren't you the gentleman in Room 417?"

"Yes."

Allan took the letter from the tray the boy in livery was holding out, and rewarded him with sixpence. From habit, he examined the envelope, and tried in vain to make out whether the blurred postmark read Paddington, Kensington or Kennington. Then he tore open the envelope and found the following communication:

> *Dear Mr. Kragh:*
>
> *Don't take offense at my giving you a bit of good advice: don't keep on wasting your money on advertisements, trying to find out about that messenger. The only result, if you continue, will be that some swindler will call on you, take your two pounds and fill you full of lies. The real messenger will never come; he held his position as messenger only one evening, and he is too honorable to be like the swindlers I have just warned you about!*

Therefore, repress your desires for further advertising!

In haste,

Sincerely yours,

DR. HAUSER, alias Ludwig Koch (alias. . . as you choose.)

P.S. Am glad you chose the Star, Daily Mail and Daily Citizen for your advertising and not the big expensive penny papers!

Allan stared in dumb astonishment at the little missive. He must be the very devil himself! He must have eyes not only in the back of his head but on all his finger-tips as well. The advertisement had contained no name; only the address of the Grand Hotel Hermitage was mentioned, yet this arch-swindler had immediately understood from whom it came. For a while Allan gave himself up to wondering about Mr. Benjamin Mirzl, puzzling over what that gentleman was intending to do in London. At last he thrust the letter in his pocket and decided to talk the matter over with the Bowlbys.

The opportunity presented itself when at about seven o'clock, he entered the hotel dining room. Mr. Bowlby and family were sitting at a table in the center of the immense room, under the shadow of the palms surrounding the ever-playing fountain of gold and marble. Beckoning Allan, he asked him to join them, an invitation which was quickly accepted. These eccentric and outspoken Americans pleased him greatly. He sat down and told them about Mr. Mirzl's latest exploits, Mrs. Bowlby all the while excitedly commenting on the whole affair: "Mr. Cray, I am willing to bet that German gets the best of these people here in London! He's a slippery customer! What do you think his idea was in returning your luggage?"

"It was in order to find out his reasons that I inserted the advertisements in the newspapers, and now you can see with what results."

"He's an arch-swindler," Mrs. Bowlby again asserted. Then she stopped short.

"Look!" she whispered. "Look there, Mr. Cray! John! I really believe the Monster is going to eat here with the rest of us. Look at their costumes, Helen!"

Allan turned quickly and saw a sight which he would not soon forget. In stately parade across the thick yellow rugs of the dining-room came a procession of five persons, the likes of which the Grand Hotel Hermitage had probably never seen before. At the head, with an inimitable bearing of inborn dignity, came a young man of thirty, a trifle stout, but whose corpulence lent grandeur to his appearance. His face was of a handsome oval with a short glossy black mustache above a discontented-looking mouth. His complexion was a dull brown, but scarcely darker than that of a sunburned sportsman. Yussuf Khan, Maharajah of Nasirabad! He was in European evening dress, but a glistening white turban rested on his head and around his neck was a thick rope of gray pearls which he seemed to bear as the insignia of some order. In the turban shone an aigrette of large sparkling emeralds. A few steps behind him came an elderly gentleman, an Englishman through and through, with fresh complexion and bristly white mustache. His eyes were a clear blue and at the moment were gleaming with excitement, the nature of which was plainly shown by his mouth, which expressed even greater dissatisfaction than had been the case with the Maharajah of Nasirabad; it was clear as day that this ostentatious entry into the Grand Hotel Hermitage dining room did not appeal to him as an English gentleman. Evidently he was Colonel Morrel, in whose charge the Maharajah had been placed. And taking into consideration the three remaining persons in the procession, his feelings could not be called unjustified. Directly behind him followed an Indian, who in the matter of years was probably of about the same age as the Colonel, but who otherwise had little in common with the latter's military appearance. His face, bearing the furrows of a life of sixty years experiences, was friendly and smiling; it was encircled by a thick gray beard, combed out to both sides, and Allan readily understood why Miss Helen with her American Presbyterian fancy had said that he looked like an archbishop. It was very evident this was the person who Mr. Bowlby had explained was the Maharajah's old court poet and teacher—Ali. Like his master he had arrayed himself in European attire, but it was clearly seen that he was wearing such a costume for the first time, and equally clear that it gave him no pleasure. The only part of his dress which seemed at all becoming was his turban. Behind him came the last two members of the escort, two dark-skinned warriors in full Indian garb, with short gilded scimitars in their brightly colored belts. Their black eyes blinked and stared about them at sight of the Grand Hotel Hermitage dining-room and its many guests. But otherwise there was not the movement of a muscle on their bearded faces as, in the wake of their master, they marched to the further end of the room.

A head waiter in scarlet coat stood by the table, bowing deeply; Yussuf Khan, Colonel Morrel and the old court poet sat down, and the black-bearded body-guard stationed themselves behind their master's chair. From around the tables in the immense dining-room came the sound of a deep breath, and then the chattering began.

Miss Bowlby was the first at Allan's table to give expression to her feelings.

"Mamma, you may say what you please, but I never saw such pearls and emeralds in all my life, not even at Tiffany's."

"Just as I expected, Helen; you are already falling in lo. . ."

"Oh, Mamma, what nonsense! Now tell me really, have you ever seen anything like them!"

Mrs. Bowlby swallowed a quantity of ice cream which probably would have permanently frozen her digestive organs had she not been a native-born American. Then she pursed up her mouth until it shot upward and almost disappeared in the shadow under her nose; thus fortified she admitted:

"No, since you must know, neither have I ever seen their like. But what good will people get out of it all if. . ."

Allan was impolite enough to interrupt.

"Colonel Morrel does not seem to be particularly pleased at having to eat here in the dining room with his charge, Mr. Bowlby."

"Not especially," admitted Mr. Bowlby. "He is English, and that pearl necklace and the black court poet are a little more than he can stomach. I'll bet a cent, Mr. Cray, that he fought against it before he took part in this triumphal procession! And I am willing to wager my last dollar against a suspender-button that if he objects often there will be a clash. Yussuf Khan seems to have a little will of his own, and it will take a woman to tame him, I imagine!"

Mr. Bowlby looked at his watch.

"Well, Susan, we must hurry if we want to get there on time. Perhaps you remember, Mr. Cray, that I told you we are going to a ball at the American ambassador's and that we won't be back much before four."

Allan hurriedly tried to cheer up Mrs. Bowlby, who seemed a bit depressed after the admission she had made to her daughter concerning the Monster.

"Do you think Mrs. Langtrey will be at the ambassador's, Mrs. Bowlby?"

"Langtrey's wife!" Mrs. Bowlby's mouth came forth from its hiding place. "She! If she is there you will see us back here in a half hour."

Mr. Bowlby laughed.

"Well, Mr. Cray, if you have nothing else to do, run up to my smoking-room and have a whiskey before you go to bed. It is at least a bit more cozy up there than down in the bar, don't you think so?"

Allan bowed. "It is really very kind of you, Mr. Bowlby. . ."

"Now don't stand on ceremony, my young friend, I like you, and I am glad to invite you. If I didn't like you I wouldn't ask you. Just go in and make yourself at home."

"But what will your servants say?"

"I will tell Henry. Well, good-bye for the present, Mr. Cray. It will be interesting to see what surprises the Maharajah will have for us in the morning!"

The American family rose and bowed to Allan, who watched them till they disappeared through the doorway. He lighted a cigarette and looked over toward the Maharajah's table. Colonel Morrel's temper had evidently not improved during dinner. His face was as red as a lobster and every now and then he directed a word, evidently not of a complimentary nature, to the aged court poet, whose knowledge of the various knives and forks used in a formal European dinner seemed rather limited.

Allan suddenly gave a start, experiencing that peculiar sensation people sometimes have when they feel someone is staring at them. He quickly turned his head to the right and to his astonishment saw at the next table Mrs. Bowlby's archfiend, Mrs. Langtrey. She sat far back in the shadow of an overhanging palm-tree; her gray eyes glistened under the big green leaves like the eyes of a cat in the dark. Had she heard what Mrs. Bowlby said? It couldn't be helped; in any case she had evidently been sitting there quite a while, for she had a cup of coffee and a liqueur glass in front of her and a cigarette between her fingers.

Allan looked at his watch. It was after half-past eight. As the Bowlbys were to be out so late, he decided to go to some variety theater or other. He could take advantage of Mr. Bowlby's invitation later on, if he wished. He motioned to the waiter, paid his bill and went out.

Two seconds later Mrs. Langtrey left.

"It will be interesting to see what surprises the Maharajah will have for us in the morning," Mr. Bowlby had said to Allan as he left. Little did he or Allan imagine the surprises that very night would bring.

CHAPTER V

THE HOLE IN THE WALL
AND THE HOLE IN THE
FLOOR

O ut of consideration—both for the place and the
exalted personage of his majesty the Maharajah—
we must call the resort which forms a frame around this,
the sixth chapter, by the name represented through the
first five words standing in the heading above. As a matter
of fact, this does not differ so greatly from the real name,
and those who know their London well can perhaps figure
out the place we mean, and where it was that Allan Kragh
experienced certain remarkable adventures during the night
of September 16.

When Allan left the Grand Hotel Hermitage shortly
after half-past eight, he had no special plans for the evening. He wandered down to Leicester Square, went into
the Empire and saw the performance, which was precisely
like all other variety performances. The performance was
in no way a disappointment to him, but as a prominent

author says about cigarettes, it was characteristic of such enjoyments—it stimulated him and left him unsatisfied. He felt the same way as he had so often during the escapades in his years of student-life, and which had cost him so much money—a disinclination to go home. He started off through the side-streets back of the Empire, wandered around at random without any feelings of fear at the types of night-life that London offered him, and without noticing the feeble lighting of the streets. If we should say that during this time he realized he was being watched or followed, it would not be quite true, and yet it is a fact, as the sequel will prove, that he was both under observation and had been followed ever since he had left his hotel, and that with diabolical skill he had been lured to just that place, where they wanted to have him. Suddenly he found himself in the street, yes, in that very street where The Hole in the Wall is situated. He stopped before the inconspicuously lighted front, which seemed as though it belonged to some little café built in continental style. Should he go home and take advantage of Mr. Bowlby's invitation, or not? Another gentleman suddenly came up, opened the door to The Hole in the Wall, and hesitated a moment on the threshold; Allan caught a glimpse of a place which looked inviting and quickly made up his mind. He walked in almost on the heels of the person who had opened the door, stopping only for a moment to look at his watch. It was twenty minutes past eleven.

The Hole in the Wall proved to be a combination of

English private bar and continental café, highly respectable in appearance. A dull polished mahogany bar in the form of a crescent extended along the right side of the room; behind it were enthroned three quietly dressed barmaids, each of them beautiful but as respectable in appearance as the bar where they were serving. The left half of the room was fitted up with wicker chairs and small tables; there was an open fireplace, not in use at the moment, and a table supplied with papers and periodicals. The lighting was low and subdued, in keeping with the general tone of the place.

For the moment all the high-legged chairs at the bar were occupied by gentlemen in dress suits and white ties, who evidently, like Allan, had dropped in on their way home from the theater or from paying some call. The man who had come in just before Allan sat at one of the small tables. Allan sat down at the table next to him, ordered whiskey, and began looking at the three pretty barmaids. One of them was of Swedish type with a rather long head, small face and pale blue eyes. Allan, who had just taken a first sip of his whiskey, suddenly felt at home and was seized with a desire to chat with someone.

He turned to his neighbor at the next table and found this person looking at him. As though anticipating Allan's wish, he leaned over smilingly and said in German:

"Excuse me if I am mistaken, but aren't we fellow-countrymen?"

Allan had been speaking nothing but English for a while now, and it seemed a pleasant change to speak another language. He shook his head:

"No, I am not German, but I speak your language. Do you think I look like a German?"

The stranger continued to eye him. "Hm, perhaps, and still, on closer thought, perhaps not. There is something not quite English about you. . . I don't know what, and it struck me."

Allan nodded.

"It isn't the first time I have been taken for a German. But the last time it was not so very pleasant."

"How was that? Was it in France?"

"No, in Germany."

"How could that happen? How could it cause you any unpleasantness to be taken for a German in Germany? Why, that is only flattering, showing you have an excellent command of the language."

"However, it was not so flattering in other respects. It was because I was taken for a well-known, yes, too well-known character, whom I am not sure whether you know or not, namely Mr. Benjamin Mirzl. Yes, I was even taken up in place of him."

"By the police? As Benjamin Mirzl!"

"Exactly, and spent almost two days under arrest on account of Mr. Mirzl. You know Mirzl then?"

"Who doesn't know about Mirzl? And since you were taken for him, now I know what he looks like."

"I imagine he changes his appearance rather often, so that probably won't do you much good. Won't you have something to drink?" added Allan, following his deep-rooted national instincts.

The stranger laughed.

"Thank you, with pleasure, Mr. Mirzl."

Allan laughed.

"I really believe you could be Mirzl just as well as I. Two whiskies and soda, please!"

His neighbor drew his chair closer. "Won't you tell me the story about Mirzl?" he asked. "That is, if it is not too painful a subject."

"No, not at all. Without doubt Mirzl is a rascal. . ."

"Of course he is. I can tell you a few things later."

"But anyway he is a rascal who knows his business—you will see that from my story, and one who has a sense of humor, too. I am not a bit angry with him because he stole all my luggage and let me take his place in jail for two days."

"Stole all your luggage? And you are not angry? You are certainly liberal minded. But go ahead with your story!"

Allan braced himself with a swallow from his glass and again repeated the story which earlier had so enlivened the Bowlby family. His companion listened with wide open eyes and now and then gave vent to an exclamation. When Allan told him about Mr. Mirzl breaking his appointment at The Leicester Lounge, the delivery of his luggage later, and his own vain attempt to trace the messenger, the stranger laughed until the bar echoed. He bent forward when Allan had finished, and with tears in his eyes said:

"One good turn deserves another. Your story is the funniest thing I have heard for ever so long. If you have time this evening, I would be glad to show you something which I think might amuse you a little, since you are a stranger in London. Would you like to join me?"

Allen looked at his watch. It lacked ten minutes of twelve.

"I thought everything closed in London about this time."

"They close latest at one, but not everywhere. There are places. . . Here, for example."

"Here! This little bar! It appears to me as though they were already making preparations to turn us out."

"They would probably have done so, too, had you been alone. But by chance I am one of the elect."

"But to stay sitting here in this little bar. . ."

"Don't judge by appearances, young man. Only among the Romans was admission to Avernus easy. Here even the admission to a tavern can be difficult."

The stranger laughed heartily at his own philological pun and went over to the counter where the barman—a stout, smooth-shaven young man who looked like a racing-stable trainer—was now alone, busy counting up the night's receipts. The three pretty barmaids had disappeared. Allan studied his new acquaintance with interest. He was a small rather thick-set man with glossy black hair and with an almost violet-blue coloring to his skin which comes from frequent shaving and is often noticed among actors. Finally he came back to Allan.

"Well, what do you say? Would you care to take a look

at the little place where the International Fire-Eaters Club holds forth?"

"International Fire-Eaters Club?" asked Allan. "Is it very strict in regard to admission?"

"Very lenient when a person is introduced by a member of the Club. Under other circumstances they are very strict. To tell the truth, it isn't really called The International Fire-Eaters Club. That is only a nick-name used among the members."

Allan arose.

"I would be glad to have you introduce me at the club," he said. "It will be a great pleasure to study the ways of the Fire-Eaters."

The stranger called out something to the man who was now closing up the entrance door to the bar. Softly whistling a tune to himself, the barman drew aside a curtain which hung at the back of the café and Allan then saw a lift, just a few feet down the corridor. The stranger motioned to him to step in first, which Allan did without it arousing his suspicions in any way. When he later thought over his night's adventures, it surprised him most of all that they did not. . . but the reader in good time will have occasion to share his surprise.

The stranger stepped in after him and pressed a button. The lift began gliding upward, so very leisurely that it even outdid the lifts at the Grand Hotel Hermitage for slowness and made it impossible for Allan to judge how high they went—the lift had been fitted with ground glass doors.

However, he did not think about that just then; another matter had come into his mind, and he turned to his companion.

"Pardon me, but how will I get out again? The bar is already closed."

The stranger smiled.

"I'll see to that. There is another exit. Now we are there."

The elevator stopped as quietly as though at the door of a sick-room. The stranger opened the ground glass doors and Allan preceded him into a large entrance hall with thick rugs on the floor. A servant in a fantastic oriental costume came hurrying forward and bowed deeply at sight of Allan's host.

"Loge number five is ready, sir," said he.

That is strange, Allan thought, had he reserved a loge in advance? Or did he come here every night?

His companion had quickly bent over toward the servant and had whispered something to him. The servant gave some sort of an answer, where upon the black-haired man gave a whistle as though in surprise, and said:

"Already there in loge number six!"

"Yes, sir. They arrived half an hour ago."

"All right. Is the passage in between open?"

"Yes, sir."

Allan's companion turned to him with a smile.

"Forgive me if I seem to act rather mysteriously," said he. "I was asking about a friend of mine."

"You must be a frequent visitor here," said Allan, "since

you had a loge reserved for you."

"Yes, I come here every now and then. Won't you take off your overcoat? It is likely to be rather warm inside."

Allan removed his coat and hat and handed them to the servant. His companion did the same and went towards a door which bore a gilded figure five. Allan followed, but half unconsciously kept an eye on the servant in oriental garb. He saw him press a button, whereupon a door opened, revealing a sort of closet in which he placed the coats that had been given him. To the right in the closet Allan caught a quick glimpse in the distance of a half-open doorway and a narrow staircase behind it. All this hardly took three seconds, yet as it later turned out, the outcome of the evening's adventure hinged upon these very three seconds. Now he was again at the side of his host. The latter turned to him with a smile.

"I take great pleasure in introducing you to the International Fire-Eaters Club," said he, and opened the door bearing the gilded number five. "Kindly walk in!"

Allen entered ahead of him. He gave a little start at the scene which greeted him. He had expected to see some little club of rather dubious character, but what met his gaze was undeniably something else.

The 'loge' where he stood was something between an ordinary box at a theatre and a tribune—it was raised a couple of feet above the floor of the large hall and was separated from it by a row of flaring lights shining into the hall. The illumination in the loge came from above through a network of Geissler's tubes, the rainbow shimmering light flowing silently down in slender streams. The walls were entirely hidden with heavy draperies. The table was spread for supper and set for two; it could, however, as well have accommodated six. Three big champagne coolers on high pedestals of silver stood at the side of the table. Oriental divans served as chairs. Beyond the row of flaring lights lay a large hall in grotesque rococo style with a smoothly polished, transparent floor. The illumination came as though from far below, filtering through the glass in rhythmic flowing waves of varicolored light, surging back and forth, lending a weird, unreal effect to the couples who were dancing there—for the hall was clearly intended as a ball-room. A throng of people, men and women in gaily colored costumes, occidental and oriental, ethnographical and purely fanciful, wide and wavy, light and airy, and even less than airy, moved over the rainbow shimmering floor to the beat of an orchestra which Allan at last discerned at the further end of the hall: the musicians in red robes which brought to mind the gowns in which the Inquisition arrayed its victims, were stationed on what looked like a black island in the gleaming sea of glass. Allan grasped his head between his hands in utter bewilderment at the scene before him. Was he awake? How could such a place have its entrance through the simple, unassuming Hole in the Wall? He turned to his companion and found that he was watching him from one of the divans, an amused smile on his face.

"The Fire-Eaters' little place impresses you?" said he.

"I have never seen anything like it in all my life," said Allan truthfully. "But how—"

"Ask no questions, my friend. Remember, a club such as ours is exclusive and does not care to have people who are strangers initiated into its secrets. Your story down there amused me, and now it amuses me to do what I can in return. But ask no questions!"

Allan bowed.

"Permit me," said he, for the second time following his deep-rooted national instincts, "permit me to introduce myself."

"Oh, what's in a name! Let me call you Mirzl, if you must have a name. One name is as good as another. Sit down and try what the club has to offer. Which do you prefer, a dry or semi-dry champagne?"

"Dry, thanks," Allan replied, and sank down on the divan opposite his odd companion. The latter continued:

"I don't know whether it interests you or not, but I can't get your adventure with Mirzl out of my head. Would it amuse you to hear the solution of it? I believe, remember, believe, that I have figured it out."

Allan's eyes opened wide with surprise and he quickly forgot both the strange place he was in and the dancing crowd on the glass floor.

"You think you have found the solution?"

"Why really, it seems to lie right at hand. I do not know whether you are aware that Mirzl made a haul in Berlin about a week ago."

"They told me about it at the police station in Cologne. It was the day before I took the express train. A hundred thousand marks in some West End hotel, wasn't it?"

"At all events, fully seventy thousand. He had been a little too daring that time, it was nip and tuck whether he would get away, and he had to leave his baggage in the lurch. Now you can well understand that he wanted if possible to get out of Germany, and he knew the police had its spies around everywhere. He did not dare to look up his confederates. If he came to the frontier and wanted to pass without luggage, he would be suspected immediately and arrested. If he tried to buy luggage of the right kind and quality, it was more than probable he would have been recognized from the descriptions which had been spread around and then in that way he would have been caught. And the ground was burning under his feet! It was a matter of hours. He had fled to Hamburg in an automobile. He had taken the express train without any plans, met you—and you know the rest. But after he was once safe in London, he no longer needed your things, and since it amuses him to be eccentric, he turned them over to you again.—But you aren't drinking anything. What do you think of my explanation?"

Allan stared at his companion with wide open eyes. The man was a veritable Sherlock Holmes! He lifted his glass to express his recognition in a toast when there came an interruption.

The draperies to the left began to wave, swelling back

and forth like the surface of the sea before some submarine disturbance and at last separated. Somebody appeared between them, like Neptune emerging from the sea, tottered a couple of steps into the loge where Allan and his companion sat, and at last with back toward them, came to a halt on a pair of none too steady legs, one hand holding tight to the draperies through which he had come. To his surprise, Allan noticed there was no wall between the loges; only the draperies separated them. Evidently these were heavy enough to deaden any noise if they were allowed to hang undisturbed, for although up to that moment he had heard no sound from the adjoining loge, there now came a murmur of voices from there. But who is this unbidden guest we have here, he was on the point of exclaiming to his companion, when suddenly the man who had come tumbling in turned his face toward them. The cry on Allan's lips sank to a whisper:

"Yussuf Khan! The Maharajah!"

It was actually and undoubtedly the Maharajah of Nasirabad and it was undoubtedly no less a fact that the Mohammedan ruler that same evening had grossly overstepped the commandments of the Prophet. Clearly he was what in good plain English might be called half-seas-over, and what in rather less polite language has a number of other appellations. It was also apparent that his slight lack of sobriety was of a cheerful, sanguine order. Now, with a careful circular movement, he turned toward Allan and his companion, made a ceremonious salaam and with dignity, although a bit indistinctly, said:

"Noble-born sahibs, a poor son of a dead Pariah begs your pardon for this intrusion in your royal t-t-te. . ."

He got no further. The exertion had been too great. He fell down limply on one of the divans, hiccoughed slightly, and finished his speech in a reclining position:

". . .te-tent. I, Yussuf, son of a thousand unworthy fore-fathers, beg your pardon."

Allan's companion had hastily risen and taken a cham-pagne bottle from one of the silver pedestaled coolers.

"Yussuf, son of heavenly born parents, condescend to drink with the most despicable of white men."

He poured out a glass, which the Maharajah, with a kindly but absent-minded smile, automatically took and emptied. He was still sitting, glass in hand, when the reddish-purple and yellow flaming draperies began to swell for the second time, on this occasion, however, more methodically than before, and then a gray bearded head and turban (the Maharajah had dropped his) showed itself through the folds, gradually followed by its owner, who turned out to be the old court poet, Ali.

He cried out something to the Maharajah, who merely answered with a wave of his champagne glass and a hearty laugh, after which he complacently stretched himself out at full length on the divan. The old court poet, who himself seemed to be in an exalted state of mind, drew the draperies aside and called into the other loge:

"Stanton Sahib, he has laid himself to rest in here! He

refuses to listen to my wise and good counsels."

The result of this cry was that a third person showed himself between the draperies, a young, light-haired and keen-eyed Englishman with the most correctly-formed sort of legs and the most clearly-cut sort of profile imaginable. He, too, seemed in brilliant spirits. With a laugh he pushed the old court poet into loge number five, then followed himself, and turning to Allan's companion with a deep oriental salaam, in a sing-song voice said:

"Noble-born Fire-Eater, forgive this obtrusiveness on the part of my two wards and my own unworthy self, son of ten generations of slaves! Salaam, noble Fire-Eater, may your shadow ever grow longer and your adversaries never have other food than dirt."

Allan watched what went on before him with mouth wide-open. In order to convince himself that he was awake he looked out on the hall where the dance still kept up its whirl around the glass floor. The sight of the dancers and the fantastic lighting effect did not contribute toward increasing his belief in his senses. Yussuf Khan here in this company! His mysterious companion from the Hole in the Wall had arisen and replied to the greetings of the young Englishman with similar oriental phrases, explaining that his tent (meaning loge number five) was absolutely unworthy of the honor conferred upon it by such distinguished strangers, whose appearance sufficiently testified to their noble birth and surpassing virtues; still if they would seat themselves in his lowly tent he would venture to propose that they empty a goblet of wine, most wretched in quality and more sour than vinegar.

Laughing heartily the young Englishman threw himself on a divan and without a murmur accepted the glass proffered him; the old court poet emptied his at a draught and arose. In spite of the wine, he was fairly steady on his legs. The Maharajah remained lying on his divan and watched all present with a smile of extreme kindliness. The old court poet raised his hands and began to speak:

"Exalted sahibs, most truly is London the most wonderful city in the world. In beauty it is beyond compare, even though it be veiled in fog, and in the virtues and kind-heartedness of its inhabitants it excels all other cities as the Koran excels all other books. Know," he turned to Allan and his companion, "that it was first to-day I arrived here in company with my young disciple, who there on his divan watches us all with a happy smile. Not until this morning did we arrive in this city where we knew nobody and now, already before the dawn of another day, my disciple and I have found many friends and have been entertained in this, the House of a Thousand Joys, all through the kind services of Stanton Sahib. This evening when we became freed of the tyranny which an old sahib, whose name I will not mention, exercises over us, my pupil and I secretly started out in the streets of London" (Allan gave a jump) "to become acquainted with the thousand pleasures which this city offers, and of which we had heard so much in the humble huts where we were born. Hardly, oh unknown sahibs, had we advanced a hundred steps before we had lost our way, bewildered by the fog which seeks to hide the beauties of London and confused by the din of the ten thousand fiery wagons. We had strayed afar like the godless who seek truth elsewhere than in the Koran (may its name forever be praised). Like those of whom my old teacher, Abdul Mahbub, sings: 'Woe to them who seek the truth elsewhere,' we had strayed far from our path when Stanton Sahib, whose name shall be famed throughout the world, saw us on the street, had mercy on us" (again Allan jumped) "and led us to this House of a Thousand Joys. Forever shall Stanton Sahib's name be praised for this deed of kindness toward two poor wanderers. In this wine which is more refreshing than the morning dew and more tempting than a woman's lips, let us drink to Stanton Sahib, most noble of Englishmen. And thereby let us remember, as the Divine Tentmaker said, it is:

> *The Grape that can with Logic absolute*
> *The Two-and-Seventy jarring Sects confute:*
> *The sovereign Alchemist that in a trice*
> *Life's leaden metal into Gold transmute.*

Exalted sahibs, let us. . ."

The old court poet could proceed no further; the exertion had been too great for him, and in the middle of his last sentence he plumped down on a divan, emptied the last drop from his glass and looked about him with an unsteady smile. Allan's companion filled the glasses and threw himself down beside the young Englishman, whom they called Stanton. Allan sat there thinking, his eyes following the dancers on the glass floor; it was more than a strange coincidence that he, who had never heard about the place before, and the two Indians, who were spending their first day in London, should all three have been taken there by friendly strangers. . . He stared at his companion, who was occupied with the young Englishman. Suddenly he gave a start at a thought which flew through his mind: had he not at the theatre in Leicester Square, seen the man who had brought him here? He could not be sure, one sees thousands of people at such a place, and there was nothing especially striking about his companion. And even then, if he had seen him at the theatre?. . . He continued involuntarily to ponder over what it was which, a few minutes ago, had struck him as being so peculiar in the fact that *he* and the two Indians should be sitting there together in the Fire-Eaters Club. Suddenly he saw the old court poet get up and on rather unsteady legs come over to him.

"Young man," said he, sitting down on the divan next to Allan, "I would confide something to you."

Allan laughingly nodded his head.

"I would confide something to you," repeated the old poet. "This wine, more refreshing than the morning dew on the hillside and more tempting than a woman's lips is even as insidious as the heart of a dweller of the plains. Ah, what profits us the women we love and the wine we drink? Both intoxications disappear with the morning, yet I am not so sure that the intoxication from this tempting wine which bubbles like a brook in early Spring, will disappear with to-morrow. I am inclined to doubt it. But if it does then will I think on what the Divine Tentmaker said:

> *And if the Wine you drink, the Lip you press,*
> *End in what All begins and ends in—Yes;*
> *Think then you are To-day what Yesterday*
> *You were—To-morrow you shall not be less.*

Young man, beware of wine and women. Take the advice of Ali, the old poet. Know that my disciple, who with a mild and happy smile is watching us from his divan, came here from across the great water to choose a bride. It is youthful folly which has led him to take such a lengthy journey for such a purpose. He is like the mountain goat who laboriously wanders down into the jungle, there to be devoured by the tigers. It shows that I have been unworthy as his teacher. Let us drink!"

Allan raised his glass.

"Venerable poet," said he, "are you aware that we are living at the same hotel?"

The old poet looked at him with eyes dimmed by wine.

"And if so?" said he. "What matters whether it be one dwelling-place or another. The more of this golden wine I drink the better do I understand the Divine Tentmaker, and when you speak of a hotel, young man, I recall those words of his:

Think, in this batter'd Caravanserai
Whose Portals are alternate Night and Day,
How Sultan after Sultan with his Pomp
Abode his destin'd Hour, and went his way.

What matter whether we live at the same hotel or not? To-morrow another will lie in the bed which still is warm from us."

"Thank goodness to-night we have champagne which still is cool enough for us," said Allan. "Your health! His Royal Highness on the divan seems to be a little tired."

"My disciple," said the old court poet, as he emptied his glass, "is not yet fully acquainted with the white sahibs' wine. Its treacherous deliciousness has overpowered him. Knowing all this, I shudder when I think about the blue-eyed white women whom he is dreaming about. Nasirabad surely will have seen its last hours when one of them encloses him in her arms. How did you know who my disciple was?"

"I have already told you that we are living at the same hotel."

It must have been shortly after this last reply that Allan also began to feel rather befuddled. In any case, it was the last bit of conversation he was clearly able to call back to mind the next day, nor was he at all sure about what happened after this while he and the others were still together. He indistinctly remembered that after he had again emptied a couple of glasses he arose to the great merriment of his queer companion, who was still talking with Mr. Stanton, and staggered through the curtains into loge number six from which Mr. Stanton and his guests had come. For a moment he stared around the loge which was fitted out in the same way as the other, and afterwards looked out to where the dance still continued on the glass floor. Then he lay down on a divan.

What he next remembered after that was his companion and Mr. Stanton looking in on him through the curtains; they looked at their watches, smiled, and drew back into loge number five; he heard the old court poet's voice, as he recited something, and he caught the sound of snoring which evidently came from Yussuf Khan.

Evidently he, too, dropped off to sleep immediately afterwards; how long he slept is uncertain, but suddenly he felt himself wide awake and, as sometimes happens in such a case, an idea was racing through his head, a sort of half premonition such as comes to one in slumber, an idea which made him sit up straight on the divan and stare before him. Was *that* what it all meant? Was that why it happened to be precisely he and the two Indians who had been introduced at that strange place? Was that the reason why his companion could give such a good explanation of Mr. Mirzl's behavior? He was confident of one thing—he must hurry if he would try to check their plan, and he was almost more confident of something else—he must act with extreme caution if he wanted to succeed. . . Still giddy from the effects of the champagne and unsteady on his feet after his sleep, he arose from the divan and as quietly as possible stole towards the door of the loge. Once there he stopped and cautiously looked over at the curtains to loge number five. They hung motionless; no sound was heard from inside. He cautiously tried the door-knob. It moved without sound. Thank goodness, at least the door was not locked, as he had feared.

He opened it as carefully as he could and peered into the hall. It was empty; nowhere was there a sign of the oriental-clad servant. With another murmured blessing to chance or Providence, he crossed the threshold, closed the door after him and tip-toed down the corridor toward the two big double doors with the elaborately grated glass panels. Quickly under way—a hasty look at his watch showed it was about two o'clock—no time to think of coat or hat—and then he discovered something which made him stagger back.

The great hall doors were locked as tightly and solidly as the gates to a prison.

For a moment he stood as though paralyzed, almost ready to go back to the loge and let matters take their course. Then he was seized with a fit of rage and with teeth tightly clenched began to search for some way to get the best of those persons there inside. He thought and thought, his eyes wandering around the hall, fully prepared at any moment to see the servant appear. The hall extended to the right and left into corridors which enclosed the loges around the ball-room with its floor of glass. Might there perhaps be an exit there? He cast aside the thought of this possibility as quickly as it had come to him. If there was a way out there it surely would be locked the same as the main exit was; without doubt the servant in the oriental clothes saw to it that no unauthorized person came in or went out and that servant was the one person whom he least of all wished to meet. He could swear to it that he had been given strict orders!—Was the game really lost? Three minutes had already gone since he had left the loge—hullo!

Suddenly he remembered something.

Again he saw the scene when he had come up with his strange companion: the servant had taken their coats and put them away in the closet, the door to which he had opened by pressing a button, and inside the closet Allan had for a minute caught a glimpse of a half-opened door which led to a back staircase. Without further thought or reckoning his chances that he would find the button to the closet door and find the other door open, Allan rushed across the hall to the door of the closet. He let his fingers quickly run over the wall where he thought he had seen the servant press; second after second went by, each punctuated by the beatings of his heart, beatings which it seemed to him should have been heard throughout the house; his fingers flew over the wall back and forth, but without result. He let his hands sink half despairingly as he stared at the wall. Then his despair changed to childlike rage; he hit the wall a blow which brought forth a dull sound and which hurt his fist; but—oh, wonder of wonders at the same moment the door opened. The next second Allan was inside the closet and had closed the door behind him, without thinking that he had no matches. He felt his way forward to the overcoats which he had seen hanging there inside, and searched them with feverish hands, one pocket after the other; the International Fire-Eaters seemed to have sworn off the use of matches. And they of all others should really have been the ones to make most use of such articles! Without bothering himself about the risk he ran in the way of broken legs and the like, he gave up his search of the overcoat pockets and felt his way along to that corner of the closet where, earlier in the evening, he had caught sight of the open door. Strangely enough, he found it almost immediately and still ajar.

He threw it open and warily took a couple of steps across the threshold, with hands outstretched. He came to an iron railing which he found enclosed a spiral staircase. He took a step back and closed the door leading from the staircase to the closet so as to leave no trace; then he started for the spiral stairs as quickly as he dared in the darkness.

If the reader has ever gone up or down a flight of dark stairs in a strange house with nothing to guide him but his sense of touch, then the same reader should have been struck by one thing: the stairway seemed as endlessly long as a sentence by some classic Latin author. If the reader has never observed this, then the same reader has never read one of the classic Latin authors. Allan Kragh, who in this respect was well circumstanced, came to the conclusion that the spiral staircase he had happened to find was fully as long as that sentence where Livy begins his reflections about the battle of Cannæ. It seemed to him as though he had been going on for aeons and while wondering whether the stairs led down to the dungeons of the Fire-Eaters Club, to Inferno, or to some station in London's underground railway, the staircase suddenly came to an end and he found himself standing in a doorway through which the gray night-light filtered in. He hurried through it as eagerly as though it led to an enchanted garden. However, it led only to a dark courtyard with a well—at least, it seemed so to him. All around him were the walls of houses, here and there with rows of dark windows, while the gable ends, far above, seemed stretching upward to the skies. He tried to pierce the darkness round about him. Had he undertaken his flight only to find himself finally closed in as though in a trap? He began to grope his way along between the objects lying on the ground of the courtyard, which narrowed down into an open passageway bending to the left. He followed the wall of the house. The passage again turned off to right angles to the way it first had taken, then turned back to the old direction and again turned off at a still different angle. Suddenly, with a cry a relief, Allan found himself before an iron grating between the high walls of two houses, of which one was overgrown with ivy. Without a moment's hesitation he climbed over the grating and landed on the other side with one trouser-leg torn. The street where he stood was short and of highly respectable appearance. At one end was an open square dimly lighted;

at the other end Allan, to his inexpressible joy, caught sight of nothing less than a hansom cab.

The cabbie submitted him to a rather careful ocular examination and demanded payment in advance before he woke his horse from its slumber and bore off in the direction of the Grand Hotel Hermitage. Gentlemen with neither hat nor overcoat at that time of night evidently aroused various feelings within him. To Allan inside the hansom it seemed as though they would never get there; street after street passed by in endless procession, house after house, sign after sign, one reddish yellow street lamp after the other. He stared at the hands of his watch as they crept forward—considerably quicker than the hansom, it seemed to him. Now and then through the trap in the roof he cried out imploringly to the cabbie. Each time, in answer, came a jerk on the reins and a weak reaction on the part of the horse. His watch showed it was ten minutes before half-past two, five minutes before the half hour, now he was sure he would come too late. . . At last the hansom turned into a broader asphalted street which he recognized, and then into Monmouth Square.

The Grand Hotel Hermitage lay silent and slumbering, with hardly a lighted window in the whole large façade; it seemed to give little warrant to Allan's fears. And still, he had hardly stepped inside the hall before he received confirmation of what he both had feared and expected.

The night porter who had opened the side entrance, stifling a yawn, stifled it completely as he caught sight of

Allan. He staggered back a couple of steps and stared at Allan as though he were a ghost.

"Who are you?" he cried.

"Number 417!" cried Allan. "Quick! Follow me! There isn't a minute to lose."

"But I saw you come in over two hours ago. . ."

"I know! I know! I will explain everything later. They have planned to commit a—have the Bowlbys come home yet?"

"No, but—"

"No buts! Upstairs with you to their apartment, and quickly, if we are to prevent what has been planned."

Without wasting time in explanations, Allan grabbed the open-mouthed porter by the arm and pulled him upstairs to the Bowlby family's suite on the second floor.

As they passed the big landing on the first floor, Allan cast a look down the corridor where lay the suite which the Bowlbys previously had and which now was occupied by the Maharajah. His assumptions were confirmed: five of Yussuf Khan's ten men were keeping watch outside the doors to the apartment. The parties concerned, then, had not been able to go this way, therefore they had—he quickened his speed up the stairs. Would he get there in time? was all he could think. Dragging the porter after him, he reached the door to Mr. Bowlby's private smoking-room—the room which, through its position and on account of other circumstances, must be the one the parties concerned had chosen for their operations. The heavy rugs in the corridor muffled the sound of his and the porter's footsteps; and rightly enough, as they reached the door and stopped for a moment before it, they heard coming from inside just exactly the sound Allan had expected: a muffled scraping as though from a file or saw. . . Allan grabbed hold of the door-knob.

The door was locked.

"What an infernal idiot I am!" Allan hotly murmured. "Porter, have you got the passkeys? Even then, what good would they do! A jemmy, and hurry!"

"A jemmy!" the porter stared at Allan as though the latter were mad.

"I tell you," Allan whispered hoarsely, "there is a criminal here at work and if he carries out his plans the hotel will be branded forever. Do you know what room lies directly underneath?"

The porter thought a second, and then his eyes opened wide.

"The Maharajah's own bedroom!" he at last mumbled under his breath.

"Where he keeps all his jewels! Do you understand now? Do you grasp the fact that the gentleman who came here two hours ago was not I but a burglar in disguise! Quick, go fetch a jemmy, and we'll catch him while there's time."

At last a light seemed to dawn upon the porter. Like an arrow he flew down the stairs and Allan stood remaining alone before the bolted door which he devoured with his eyes.

That cursed Mirzl! If Allan had not happened to strike

on the idea he did at the Fire-Eaters Club, then he would now have the 'honor' of the burglary on his shoulders and. . .

Allan never completed his thought. All at once, without his having heard a sound, the door before him was thrown open; somebody in evening dress who looked like him grabbed him by the arms, twirled him around as though he were a child, and threw him into the room in front of which he had been waiting. He was simply slung in like some dead object and did not even have time to think of rising before the electric light in the room went out, and he found himself in a darkness of black abysmal night. His head beat and whirred as though it were a watch maker's shop and his eyes saw more stars than have ever appeared on a bottle of brandy. At last he was on his legs again and groped his way as quickly as he could to the door. It was locked. He threw himself against it, but it did not give way. He succeeded in finding the electric switch and turned it round and round as though he were winding a clock, but not a spark of light came. At last he heard quick steps outside, a rattling at the door, and then the porter's voice:

"Have you got him in there? Did you turn off the lights at the main switch?"

Allan succeeded in suppressing the words which were trembling on his tongue.

"For Heaven's sake," he yelled, "don't let him out down below! Bolt the doors! Call the police! He has locked me up in here!"

He heard the porter as he hurried down the stairs, not even stopping long enough to turn on the electric light switch to the apartment, and an eternity went by while he, foaming with impatience, danced up and down before the bolted door; now and then he made a further attempt to force it open, but always without result. Perhaps ten minutes had passed, ten centuries it seemed to him, when for the second time he heard steps outside, this time of several people. Suddenly the room was filled with light and a key was turned in the lock. He himself pulled the door open and outside found the porter, breathless from excitement, and with him two policemen.

Allan wanted to begin explaining and asking questions, but a cry from one of the policemen forestalled him.

"Gawd! Attempted burglary, sure as fate! Look!"

Allan turned in the direction where the policeman was pointing. If he had needed any further confirmation of the correctness of his suppositions, he was about to receive it.

A hole, perhaps two feet in diameter, gaped before them in the floor, at the side lay a closed umbrella and a pile of shavings and bits of mortar. He stared blankly at the umbrella until one of the policemen hurried over to the hole in the floor and lifted up the umbrella. He opened it; it was found to contain a lot of shavings, bits of plaster and mortar. The policeman nodded:

"The usual trick, so the mortar won't fall into the room below! His rope ladder he succeeded in taking with him."

At last Allan found his tongue again.

"Has he escaped then?"

The porter nodded gloomily.

"He turned off the lights both at the main switch and at the switch to this apartment. They are both in the hall by the stairs. I was down in the office calling up the police. When the lights went out I ran up the stairs—you needn't look at me so, sir; what else would you have done? In such cases people know best what to do after it has happened. I noticed nothing in the dark before I turned on the main switch the switch to the apartment here. At just that moment I saw somebody disappear down the stairs. I rushed after. . ."

"Didn't he go *before then*?" cried Allan. "Why did he wait so long?"

"Ask somebody else, sir. I rushed after him, but it was too late. He was out of the hotel and in a taxi, which was waiting a little way up the street, before I was able to cry out. Just then the policemen came. . ."

One of the policemen referred to interrupted him.

"We will have to make out a report," said he.

"Is that necessary?" mumbled the porter. "The Maharajah—think of the hotel's reputation!"

"We will keep everything secret, if you yourselves do the same."

Still half bewildered from his many experiences Allan told the police what he knew. They shook their heads at his tale about the Fire-Eaters Club.

"Are you sure you were sober, sir? No offense intended,

but. . ."

Allan repeated his description with a certain vehemence.

"And the address of the place, sir?"

Allan took a step back. He had been in such a hurry, Lord knows, in getting away from the place in question, that he had absolutely forgotten to take a look at the name of the street where it lay.

"Because you said, did you not," continued the policeman quietly, "that this Indian prince who owns, or did own, the jewels in the room below, was there when you left?" Allan nodded silently. Good Lord, what would those rogues do to the Maharajah when they found out that their other plans had miscarried—if such proved to be the case?

"The Maharajah was there, when I succeeded in getting away," he stammered at last. "Think, if by succeeding in preventing their attempt at burglary I have simply. . ."

"Whether or not you succeeded in preventing the burglary, we will hardly find out to-night, or will you take the responsibility, porter, of letting us into the Maharajah's apartment?"

The porter shook his head energetically. After a few more questions the policeman slipped his notebook into his pocket.

"Leave the room undisturbed. The detectives will come early to-morrow, if not before," he said, and left with his fellow officer.

Allan staggered up the stairs to his room after asking the porter to inform Mr. Bowlby in a few careful words about what had happened. He was dead tired from all the champagne, excitement, and his struggle with Mirzl—if it had been Mirzl.

If he had felt any doubts on that subject they would, however, have been dispelled when he reached his Egyptian sepulchre, number 417. The room was brightly lighted when he opened the door, and the first thing he saw was his one and only trunk where, excepting when actually travelling, he very impractically was in the habit of leaving his money under lock and key—he had not yet formed the wise habit of depositing his money with the porter of the hotel where he was stopping. The cover, which was secured by two good padlocks, stood wide open and the contents of the trunk—a few small articles, among them the box which held his money—lay around in absolute disorder. Seized with a dire foreboding he rushed over to the trunk and quickly opened the box in question—an artistic little bit of silverware which he had once bought in Denmark. It had contained eleven thousand six hundred Swedish crowns that morning. Of these there now remained five thousand six hundred.

Several minutes went by before he collected his thoughts sufficiently to look around the rest of the room; and then the first thing to meet his eyes was a letter leaning against the electric light on the table by his bed. He tore it open with a cry of rage:

Dear Mr. Kragh:

Perhaps you will find my conduct to-night illogical and ungentlemanly. Illogical because I was well disposed toward you on account of a service you did me in Germany; ungentlemanly because I am depriving you of six thousand Swedish crowns. Parenthetically I might add that it was through chance I found them; it really had been my intention simply to write you a few lines here in quietness and peace. But let me tell you this: you have thwarted my plans to-night, and a person who thwarts me does not go unpunished. The punishment for your first misdemeanor is a fine of six thousand crowns—half your fortune in the trunk. Should the offense be repeated—but I am sure that you are wise enough not to repeat it.
In haste,

DR HAUSER (alias Ludwig Koch, alias Benjamin Mirzl)

CHAPTER VI

A Disappearance And Other Matters

It was Mr. Bowlby who awoke Allan the next morning a little after half-past eight. Allan sprang up in bed, still half asleep and certain that it was Mr. Benjamin Mirzl who had come back for the rest of the money.

"You, Mr. Bowlby!"

"Yes, I, my young friend. I received your message from the porter when I came home last night shortly after four o'clock. Forgive me for so unceremoniously paying you a call in your bedroom—hang it all, but it surely is one of the smallest ones I have ever seen! But you can easily understand my curiosity! A hole in my smoking-room large enough for a pitfall to catch Indians! The room full of detectives who have questioned me and who intend to question you, and a queer, crazy sort of story which the night porter told me about *two* gentlemen in 417. I expected you would be down long before this, but Helen just told me that you never get up before lunch."

"Miss Bowlby is too severe in her judgment. If you

don't mind, I will get dressed and then I will try to tell you all about it. But you know, of course, that for the present everything must be kept secret?"

"The detectives mentioned some nonsensical thing about the Maharajah. . ."

"It was nothing nonsensical, I fear, Mr. Bowlby."

Allan jumped out of bed and unconcernedly began his ablutions before the eyes of the American, in the meantime relating his evening's adventures. The description of the Fire-Eaters Club brought forth a series of whistles on the part of Mr. Bowlby worthy of an express train tearing along. When Allan came to the story about his flight and how Mirzl succeeded in fooling him and the porter, he interrupted him with a cry:

"But he must be a very devil, that man Mirzl! Talk about coolness! That was the most daring thing I ever heard of in my life!"

"Wait a moment with your praise!" said Allan. "What do you think the man did after he had locked me in the smoking-room and turned off the electric light switches?"

"Ran away, of course."

"Ran away! Then you don't know Mirzl. He came up here to my room and sat down to write a letter, warning me not to interfere again in his affairs—"

"The deuce you say?"

"And when by chance he noticed that my trunk was locked and it looked as though it might contain something of value, he opened it. Remember, the porter all this time was standing down stairs ringing up the police! In the trunk I had my travelling money, eleven thousand Swedish crowns and a trifle more."

"You are mighty careless! And he took it?"

"He took a little more than half. Then he sat down and wrote this letter here."

Allan, not without a certain pride, handed Mr. Mirzl's letter to Mr. Bowlby. The American read it through slowly, letting out the while a new series of deafening express train whistles.

"Of course you called up the police!"

"The police! Why not an orphan asylum and beg for a nurse? I lay down and went to sleep."

An expression of genuine respect came over the American's face.

"Well! I must say. . .!"

He stared at Allan while the latter put on his coat. Allan opened the door for him and they went downstairs. Mr. Bowlby repeated:

"I must say! And don't you intend to report the matter now?"

"Since the detectives are here, I will of course report the affair to them, but only as a matter of form."

"Mirzl seems to have gained your respect!"

Allan nodded affirmatively. At that moment they caught sight of Mrs. Bowlby and Miss Helen, who were sitting near the staircase in the hall on the second floor. Mrs. Bowlby, more parrot-like than ever in a bright green costume, greeted Allan with a little shriek which in no way was unworthy of the abovementioned species of bird.

"*Mister* Cray! Well! So this is the way you carry on at nights when you are out of my sight! A big hole in the floor, and detectives flocking around it like flies around an open jar of marmalade. They wouldn't even let me get anywhere near it. They evidently thought I intended to hop down into the Monster's bedroom. —Well, what have you got to tell us? Sit down and let us hear, but *everything*, understand. Of course you went to some Horrible Place? *Was* it you, who made the hole in the floor?"

"If you had come into Mr. Bowlby's smoking room between half-past twelve and half-past two you surely would have thought so, Mrs. Bowlby."

Allan started to tell his story for the second time. Mrs. Bowlby did not honor his description of the Fire-Eaters Club with express whistles as had her husband, but her comments were just as expressive for all that. When Allan concluded telling about Mr. Mirzl's exploits, she started in:

"Yes, the man of course is a scamp. But, I can tell you, I would a thousand times rather see the Monster get caught than him."

"I, for my part, would six thousand times rather see Mirzl caught," Allan confessed.

"Think, that on his *first* evening here in London he would go out to such a Place," the old lady continued accusingly. "Of course he was in the company of Ladies— don't try to deny it, I won't believe you anyway. Of course, although he has a house full and *more* than full of them there at home. And, of course, it is terribly wrong of you to go to such a Place, but a married man, a man who is a *hundred and fifty* times married. . . And that old gray-bearded wretch. . ."

Allan courageously interrupted her. "Haven't they come home yet, Mrs. Bowlby?"

"They! They won't come home in a hurry, you may be sure of that. I know men."

Mr. Bowlby, while he listened to Allan tell his story, had absent-mindedly been breaking the rules of the hotel by smoking. Now he suddenly took his cigar out of his mouth and by entering into the conversation, prevented Allan from expressing his fears of what now would be the fate of the Maharajah as the burglary had miscarried.

"There are two things," said he, "which I cannot understand, no matter however cunning that German and his gang may be. Of course they shadowed you from the moment you left the hotel, but how could they lure you into just that place where the Maharajah was?"

"Hm, Mr. Bowlby, there is nothing so extraordinary about that. I happened to walk into that café in company with his confederate and he spoke to me. That was mere chance. But if I had gone into any other place the result would have been the same. If necessary they would not have hesitated to use force."

"Well, I can admit that much. But there is something else, too. I can realize they would keep a watch on the

Maharajah both indoors and out. But *you* have had nothing to do with either the Maharajah or any of his party, and your room is on the fourth floor. Yesterday evening I asked you to have a whiskey upstairs in my place. How in the devil did they find out about that and make use of it? That is what I want to ask. There was no one near the table where we were as far as I could see."

"And how could they have found out that we were to be away half the night, Papa?"

"There is nothing strange about that, Helen dear, if they had spies in the hotel. But when I invited this young man up to my room there was not a soul in the vicinity as far as I can remember, and I have a mighty good memory."

"They didn't *need* to know all about that, Papa. They could have made the attempt on the jewels in any case, as far as I can understand. They had seen Mr. Cray and us going around together, they had shadowed him the whole evening as he himself says, and got him out of the way, and then this man Mirzl dressed up to look like him."

Miss Bowlby got no further in her explanation. Allan had jumped up in his chair and grabbed Mrs. Bowlby by the wrist. The old lady started up with her head on one side, like a parrot in fighting mood.

"What are you doing, sir? Do you think you are still at that Place?"

"Mrs. Bowlby! You were certainly correct in what you said about your countrywoman! Now I understand, or at least believe I understand! Aha! They belonged together then at all events."

"My countrywoman? Who? What do you understand?"

"Mrs. Langtrey! Now I remember. Just after you had risen from dinner last night, I happened to look over to my right, and there, deep in the shadow of the palm-leaves, sat Mrs. Langtrey. You know before you left you said some. . . hm, rather open-hearted things about how great the possibilities were of her going to the ambassador's ball. When I caught sight of her she looked like a tigress. You may be sure she heard not only what you said about her but also what Mr. Bowlby said to me about having a whiskey upstairs. Your husband even promised he would tell the servant I was coming. It was she, who—You know I saw her and Mirzl together at the station in Hamburg, although at that time I did not think they knew each other. . ."

Allan had not come to an end when Mrs. Bowlby flew up from her chair like a hawk from its nest and with quickly flapping wings rustled down the stairs. Her eyes gleamed with triumph. Mr. Bowlby philosophically shrugged his shoulders and lighted a new cigar. Allan, who had to laugh at the old lady's combative manner, was on the point of going into further explanations when one of the hotel attendants came up to him.

"The inspector is in Mr. Bowlby's smoking room, and would like to question you, sir."

Allan followed him to the room which the day before had been the scene of Mr. Mirzl's defeat and his own. It was not so completely filled with detectives as Mrs. Bowlby's words had given him reason to expect, but at all events it did contain the respectable number of four of Sherlock Holmes' colleagues. One of these, who in appearance most clearly resembled his famous thin colleague, was also evidently the inspector, because it was he who, as Allan entered, asked him to sit down and then began to question him. He sat at a little table, littered over with documents and mysterious things in envelopes and boxes. Allan recalled his memories of Sherlock and drew the inference that the envelopes and boxes contained the 'clues' they had found. The thin man turned over a couple of pages in his notebook and put his fountain pen in order.

"You are Mr. Allan K-r-a-g-h?"

He spelled the surname, evidently unwilling to fall into any phonetic trap.

"Yes. From Sweden."

"From Sweden, yes. You are living in 417?"

"Yes."

"It was you who came home at about half-past two last night, and together with the night porter tried to surprise the thief?"

"It was I."

"Tell me how you happened to have the idea that a thief was here."

Allan, for the third time that morning, related his story in the same form as he had before. He described his visit to The Hole in the Wall, the stranger who had spoken to him, the lift which had carried them up to the Fire-Eaters Club, the Maharajah's entrance in their loge and how he suddenly had formed the suspicion which made him leave the club as he did. Evidently the inspector had already heard the story from the policeman who had come to the hotel the night before, for he kept referring to a paper which he had beside him. Now and then he made a note. He let Allan finish his story before he began to question him.

"Will you describe, as well as you can, the man who spoke to you in The Hole in the Wall?"

"He was rather thick-set, with a square face, glossy black hair and had a bluish-violet shimmer to his chin and cheeks. Not much to help you in tracing him, I am afraid. He was in evening dress. He said he was German, and at least he spoken German fluently."

"You speak German yourself?"

"Yes."

"And the man who was together with the Maharajah?"

"He was an Englishman, at least the others said so; they called him Stanton. He had light hair, keen eyes and made a very correct impression in his whole appearance—an unusually typical example of his countrymen, if I may say so."

The inspector looked through his papers for a moment.

"May I ask a question, Inspector?"

"What is it?"

"The Maharajah has not come back yet?"

"No. We have been trying to get on his track since four o'clock this morning, but our investigations must be as circumspect as possible, both for the Maharajah's sake as well as that of the hotel. What pleases us is that the robbery was prevented."

"How do you know that?" Allan burst out.

The inspector smiled for the first time. "We know it through a—hm—a peculiar incident. But how is it, haven't you a loss to report on your own account?"

Allan jumped in earnest. That broke all the records for keenness on the part of detectives he had ever read or even dreamed about! Had this thin Inspector deduced his loss of money from the way he tied his shoe-laces or some spot or other on the left side of his sleeve? He stared at the Inspector in dumb amazement. With a smile on his face, the latter drew out a paper from the pile in front of him and handed it to Allan.

"Please read it," he said. "It came by the first mail this morning."

Allan took the paper and hurriedly read the lines in the all too well-known handwriting.

To Scotland Yard:

Mr. Allan Kragh of Sweden, stopping at the Grand Hotel Hermitage, Room 417, had stolen from his room last night, between the hours of half-past two and three, the sum of six thousand Swedish crowns (in thousand crown notes).

The perpetrator of the theft begs leave to point out that this constitutes the lightest punishment it seemed reasonable to impose on Mr. Kragh for his

*interference in the other affair the same night at
the Grand Hotel Hermitage.*

*In case Mr. Kragh has not yet reported the
matter, I desire to inform you of the fact herewith.
Mr. Kragh is an amiable young man worthy of
your deepest consideration.*

In haste,

BENJAMIN MIRZL.

P. S. Lack of time prevents the insertion of aliases.

The Inspector smilingly watched the expression on
Allan's face as he read the note.

"Evidently you don't know Mirzl, since you seem so
surprised," he said.

"Don't know him? Oh, yes, I do, somewhat, as you can
see from the letter itself. And you? Do you know him?"

"I can answer as you did, somewhat! He made life here
in London a bit of hell for us three years ago—the ten
burglaries in Regent Street, the carrying off of the Ascot
cup, the conjuring away of the crown jewels of Ireland
and a dozen other offences, which to be sure we could not
directly lay at his door, yet we could almost swear he had
committed. Yes, we do know Mr. Mirzl a bit. Thank goodness, he left the country after the Ascot affair and proceeded
to make matters unpleasant for the authorities in his own
land. Now, it seems, he has got tired of that and—"

"And would probably never have been able to cross the

border if I had not helped him!"

Allan could not resist playing his little trump. The detectives listened in silence to the description of his adventures on the express train. When he had finished the Inspector said:

"Let me give you a bit of good advice: don't mention your little tale east of the Rhine; I doubt whether they would decorate you with any medals for that affair."

"And the sort of thanks I get from Mirzl himself, you have seen. Since you know that he is at the bottom of it all and you have made such a thorough investigation of the matter, tell me, have you any hopes of finally catching him this time?"

"Officially, officially," nodded the Inspector, "we are extremely hopeful. But for the moment, what weighs on our hearts almost more heavily than the whereabouts of Mr. Mirzl is the whereabouts of his Royal Highness, Yussuf Khan."

The Inspector, with wrinkled brow, stopped and time and again tapped his notebook on the table. Allan stifled a mumbled oath that was finding its way up from the bottom of his heart. At that moment the door was thrown open and a white-mustached, irate old gentleman rushed into the room. Allan recognized him as the Maharajah's European adviser, Colonel Morrel.

"Well!" he cried. "Any news? Any clues?"

The Inspector shook his head.

"We hope that later on in the day—" he began.

"Later on in the day, later on in the week, later on in Hell!" roared the old Colonel and stamped on the floor until the room echoed. "You must, do you hear, you must get hold of him before to-night. We are to be received by the Home Secretary for India, that civilian pu—hm, at five o'clock. Tea, and Heavens knows what! You *must* have him here by then, do you hear? Otherwise I'll raise—"

"If I were in your place, Colonel, I would send word to the Home Secretary for India that you cannot come. I surely would. If we entertained any doubts about Benjamin Mirzl being at it again, they have faded away after this young man's story, and Mirzl, who stole the Irish crown jewels certainly would not hesitate to steal a reigning prince—"

"This young man, here! Who the deuce is this young man, here?" The Colonel stared at Allan as though he were a little drummer boy.

"Mr. Allan K-r-a-g-h," spelled out the Inspector from a paper before him, "of Sweden."

"Sweden, Norway, it's all the same to me. Who the deuce is Mr. Allan K-r-a-g-h?"

"The gentleman who last saw his Royal Highness in the mysterious club which you have heard mentioned, Colonel!"

"Ah-h-h!" The Colonel roared like a mortally wounded tiger. "It was you, sir, who enticed his Highness through the streets and alleys up to that infernal place, where he now lies robbed and murdered. It was you, don't try to deny it! It was you!"

Allan, who had risen from his chair, had all he could

do to keep from laughing. The Colonel had turned a deep Burgundy red with rage at the thought of Allan's piece of villainy. Verily, it paid to do good deeds and save the crown jewels of an Indian prince from being stolen! It seemed to be as grateful a piece of business as helping a certain person to escape from his own country when it had grown too hot for him—the same person, by the way, who wanted to steal the jewels in question!

"It was not I who lured his Highness away or enticed him up—"

"It was you! I can see it in your face. What is the sense of standing there, denying it!"

"It was *not* I," said Allan, afraid the Colonel would have a stroke through these repeated denials. "You refer to an accomplice of Mirzl's whom you have already heard the Inspector speak about. I myself was enticed into the club. . ."

"Ha, ha! Ha, ha, ha! Enticed! Arrest him, Inspector! Why, the devil take me, you can see and hear it was he."

"I was myself enticed into the club by another confederate of Mirzl's. We were liberally entertained with wine, I, as well as the Maharajah and the old poet, who after a while came into the box where I was sitting. May I ask, Colonel, whether you know any one by the name of Stanton?"

"Stanton? Stilton? Who the devil is Stanton?"

"He was the man who lured his Highness to that place."

"Ha, ha! Of course! Inspector. . ."

"After a while I succeeded in escaping and fortunately arrived here in time to prevent the burglary which was being carried out by the great Mirzl himself. He had disguised himself to resemble me and. . ."

"My Lord, Inspector, do you hear or are you deaf? Can you swallow any more of this fellow's lies without their choking you? Disguised to resemble him! May I drop dead if I ever heard the likes of that! It *was* he, of course it was he, as I have been yelling to you for an hour!"

"My dear Colonel, let me ask you one thing: Can a person be on both sides of a door at the same time?"

"Certainly, if one wishes to!"

"It is, namely, the only possible way to account for this young man first being seen by the night porter making his escape through the entrance to the hotel, and then, when the porter and police came upstairs, his being found grossly mishandled here in this room."

"Then he must have climbed up here again through the hole in the floor!"

"And have passed the guards at the Maharajah's bed-chamber, and climbed through the hole in the floor without a ladder, merely to meet the police here?"

This finally silenced the Colonel. The possibilities, as the Inspector explained them, for Allan to have been the culprit, seemed too slight even for his ready imagination. He sank down on a chair and wiped his forehead with his handkerchief.

"But, Lord help us all!" he groaned. "The Home Secretary for India expects us for tea and goodness knows what else at five o'clock! And my reputation! And the

Government in India!"

"You should be thankful to this young man," said the Inspector gently but firmly. "He at least prevented the jewels being stolen. It came within a hair's-breadth of happening. You surely ought to be thankful."

The Colonel turned a blood-shot eye on Allan which showed no special expression of thankfulness. He murmured something inaudible, jumped up and rushed out through the door.

Allan and the Inspector exchanged smiles. At that moment the door was thrown open and Mrs. Bowlby burst in like a bomb. She caught sight of Allan and planted herself in front of him.

"Have you told them about Langtrey's wife?" she cried, and kept turning first to Allan and then to the Inspector. "Have you?"

"Langtrey's wife?" asked the Inspector. "Who is she?"

"A terrible woman," cried Mrs. Bowlby triumphantly. "Terrible! It is she who is back of the whole business, mark my words."

"May I ask one of you to tell me all about it, but as explicitly as possible?" said the Inspector, and seized his pen.

"May I, Mrs. Bowlby?" said Allan.

Mrs. Bowlby nodded while she triumphantly held herself ready to supply all necessary marginal notes.

"I remembered something just before the inquiry, Inspector, which set me to thinking. Evidently, through spies in the hotel, Mirzl and his accomplices have kept a strict watch over everything that goes on here. They may perhaps have been some of the servants, chambermaids, waiters or some of the numerous pages. Through them they have kept informed about conditions, as well as the fact that I was on friendly terms with the Bowlby family who occupy the suite of rooms just above his Highness' apartment. They found out that Mr. Bowlby and family were to be out until a late hour last night. This affair had been decided upon since Friday and they immediately made their plans. Whether under normal circumstances the project would have taken the form it did, that is, Mirzl impersonating *me*, is of course not certain, although it is perhaps likely. But now, it happened that before leaving the dining-room last night, Mr. Bowlby very kindly said I was welcome to go upstairs to his smoking-room later if I wished, and have a whisky and soda. That was at eight o'clock and Mr. Bowlby also promised to tell his servant that I might come up. Does the significance of these details strike you? At the time, we were alone at the table, none of the servants were near us. If Mirzl at the last moment found out about that, it no doubt settled his choice of disguise. But how could he have learned about it? As I have already said, none of the servants were near us. But shortly after Mr. Bowlby and his family left I happened to look to the right of our table and there, well-screened by shadows from the palms which decorate that part of the dining room, sat an American lady, who according to Mrs. Bowlby, has a rather unsavory reputation. She comes of good family, but left America several years ago and is supposed to have joined forces with an adventurer here in Europe. Her name is Mrs. Langtrey."

"And to-day," Mrs. Bowlby cried with a shrill flute-like tone, "at half-past seven this morning, Mrs. Langtrey disappeared from the hotel, after receiving a local telegraph message!"

CHAPTER VII

THE ADVENTURES OF
MYNHEER VAN SCHLEETEN

M ynheer Jan van Schleeten's life had had its changes; the pleasant part of this for Mynheer van Schleeten was that they had always been part of an ascending curve. Unknown in the beginning, he had become a celebrity throughout Europe, from poverty he had risen to wealth, from wealth to more wealth. In the year that Yussuf Khan of Nasirabad made his first visit to this part of the world, Mr. van Schleeten was its most famous jewel specialist. As Mr. Bowlby had informed Allan, it was he who made the diadem which the French republic sent to the Empress of Russia on a certain notable occasion, and there were a score of similar commissions to his credit. His main office was in Amsterdam but his calling demanded his presence almost as much in Berlin, Paris and London as in his home city. In all of these places he had branches or agents.

At the end of August of the abovementioned year (while in Berlin on a commission for a financier whose name began with B and who was later raised to the peerage) he received a letter from his London agent stating that a certain Colonel Morrel wished his services for his charge, the Maharajah of Nasirabad. Mynheer van Schleeten, who had never had any dealings with oriental princes, but of whose jewels he had heard so much the more, hastened to accept the proposal especially as it was accompanied by very flattering terms. He imparted his joy to the newspapers which, through several news items, rejoiced with him. There were to be new settings for the Maharajah's jewels as well as various other alterations. The young prince was somewhat eccentric and had become tired of things which had kept the same appearance for the last thousand years.

Early in September, Mynheer van Schleeten left for Hamburg where he had a small agency; and on the same day that Mr. Allan Kragh arrived in the city from Sweden, Mr. van Schleeten left on the morning express bound for Paris where he had a little matter of business to attend to, which when settled would easily permit him to reach London at the appointed time.

Mynheer van Schleeten's adventures began on the express train.

Being a Hollander he was phlegmatic; the successes he had experienced during his approaching sixty years of life had contributed to increase this phlegmatic Dutch temperament. He seldom became excited; he had only two passions, both of which he gratified in a suitable manner. The first, which increased as the years passed on, was old Bordeaux of pleasing body; the second, which decreased a bit as the years passed on, was young women of pleasing body. In his youth Mynheer van Schleeten had partaken of sundry gay little suppers with the other sex; his phlegmatic temperament, however, had hindered him from indulging in these little suppers often enough to deprive him of the ability to enjoy a good dinner. In later years Mr. van Schleeten dined more frequently than he supped. This was also manifest from his appearance; his nose was large, aquiline, and with time had begun to assume the color of that good French wine in which he so loved to see it reflected. Through these libations his yellowish-gray mustache had flourished like a tree planted at the side of a stream; and nowadays, when Mr. van Schleeten drank, it hung over his Bordeaux glass like tufts of grass over the banks of a brook.

Mention has been made of the preceding facts in order to explain Mynheer van Schleeten's adventures while on the express train between Hamburg and Cologne and later on.

Directly after Mr. van Schleeten had taken his seat in a first class compartment on the express—following his usual custom, a place by the window facing the engine—a lady entered. For a moment she looked at Mr. van Schleeten, who in turn looked at her. He came to the conclusion that she was young, of rather pleasing body and, although a bit haughty in manner, good looking, and that therefore during the frivolous period of his life he would have had no objection to a little supper with her. What impressions she received from her scrutiny of him are unknown; however, they were evidently satisfactory, for she deposited her handbags on the rack and herself on the seat directly opposite Mr. van Schleeten. Then the train started and Mr. van Schleeten became engrossed in the study of his morning papers, thus showing his phlegmatic nature.

It was not until they reached Bremen that anything happened.

Scarcely had the train come to a stop in the station when Mr. van Schleeten heard steps in the corridor and saw the door to the compartment opened by a young man who appeared to be searching for someone. Mr. van Schleeten noticed that the young man was of rather prepossessing appearance, but since he greatly disliked having too many people travel in the same compartment with him, he looked at the young man with a determined, stern and forbidding expression on his face, as much as to say, "Go into the next compartment, my young friend!" Without paying the least attention to this, the young man calmly sat down on the seat beside Mr. van Schleeten, thereby robbing the latter of all chance to stretch himself out and indulge in a little nap after lunch. Mr. van Schleeten repeated his stern and forbidding glance and added a portion of well-bred astonishment at such conduct. Alas! he perceived that this glance was lost on the young man (who, moreover, was travelling without luggage): he was completely engrossed in devouring with his eyes Mr. van Schleeten's beautiful vis-à-vis; she on her part seemed to have fallen asleep. Mr. van Schleeten made some mental comments concerning the young people of to-day, and after a while resumed his study of the morning papers.

The next incident happened after the train had speeded some half-hour further on its journey. The compartment door was again suddenly opened, this time to Mr. van Schleeten's satisfaction, to admit the guard, who wanted the tickets. The young man produced his own which to the disappointment of Mr. van Schleeten seemed to be in order. The guard turned to Mr. van Schleeten, examined his ticket, and then, to attract the attention of the young lady who sat opposite Mr. van Schleeten, coughed an apologetic "Gnädige" a couple of times. It seemed to be in vain. She continued sleeping. After apparently a moment's consideration the young man leaned forward and softly tapped Mr. van Schleeten's vis-à-vis on the knee.

The effect was instantaneous. The young lady started up from her seat, threw an outraged and indignant look at the young man, stared about her, handed the guard her ticket and then burst forth into a tempestuous flood of English words: How dared that young man do such a thing? What did he mean by it? Couldn't a person travel in Europe (she was an American, then) without being insulted? To Mr. van Schleeten her indignation seemed somewhat exaggerated when he thought of other ladies evidently of equally good family, whom he had tapped and not merely on the knees; but as he reflected that she, through her unusual manner, might perhaps drive the young man away from his (Mr. van Schleeten's) seat, he took good pains not to check her. Suddenly she turned to him:

"Sir, did you see whether this young man took still further liberties with me while I slept?"

"I do not know," said Mr. van Schleeten diplomatically, still thinking of his little after-luncheon nap. "I was reading my newspaper."

"Very well!"

She resumed her attack on the young man, who in the beginning had listened, absolutely dumbfounded, but now attempted an explanation. She interrupted him curtly:

"How *dare* you speak to me?"

This was too much for her adversary. To Mr. van Schleeten's delight he arose from his seat and disappeared down the corridor. At that moment Mr. van Schleeten experienced a certain feeling of remorse that he had helped put him to flight; it would hardly be pleasant travelling alone with such a supersensitive little shrew. The young man was hardly outside the door, however, before her expression changed as quickly as an April sky and she beamed on Mr. van Schleeten with the sunniest smile in the world.

"I was perhaps, a bit quick-tempered," she said, "but I cannot endure the obtrusiveness of such young whippersnappers."

She placed an accent on "such young whippersnappers" which affected Mr. van Schleeten pleasantly. He noticed she had strong white teeth, and that her eyes, when she smiled, were singularly attractive. In color they were gray; gray had, of late years, become Mr. van Schleeten's favorite color for eyes, since he had looked too deep in far too many that were blue and black, and had been made to suffer for it.

"Madame," he said, "that young man's boldness was intolerable."

After a while they were deep in an interesting conversation which was interrupted by the dining car waiter who poked his head in their compartment and notified them that dinner was being served. Although Mr. van Schleeten by this time felt he would have no objection whatsoever to a little supper with his vis-à-vis, yet he pushed the thought aside for the moment and proposed that they should have dinner together. She accepted graciously:

"Of course, with the understanding that I shall pay for myself."

Mr. van Schleeten bowed.

It was several hours after dinner, which had passed in the pleasantest manner possible with fine old Bordeaux, before Mr. van Schleeten again caught sight of the young man who had threatened to rob him of his little doze after luncheon. He bore no grudge against the young lady who actually had robbed him of that pleasure; she had furnished him with so many other pleasures through her highly flirtatious conversation. It was at the station in Cologne. Mr. van Schleeten and the young American, whose name he now knew was Mrs. Langtrey, gave a start in the midst of an interesting discussion on the advisability of coeducational schools, as they heard excited voices in the corridor. They looked out and saw the young man, who had provoked them both to anger, disappear in company with a police officer and a man in civilian clothes, who Mr. van Schleeten realized was a detective. Mr. van Schleeten looked at Mrs. Langtrey; Mrs. Langtrey looked at him and cried:

"Do you see, just as I said! I seem to feel when I am near a criminal!"

While Mr. van Schleeten expressed to her his admiration for this intuitive feeling, he admitted to himself that *his* feelings for her were not at all of a telepathic nature.

On their arrival in Paris at half-past ten in the evening it was very natural that they should put up at the same hotel. Mr. van Schleeten recommended a quiet family hotel in the neighborhood of the Church of the Madeleine and she quickly accepted his choice. According to her statement, she had never been in Paris before. She had crossed on one of the Hamburg-American Line boats and was only travelling to forget her grief over the death of her first husband, and to escape a troublesome suitor who imagined that she was in love with him.

Mr. van Schleeten was quite ready even on that first night in Paris, to help her forget all grief, but no opportunity offered itself. After a cup of tea Mrs. Langtrey disappeared into her room.

Two days later they went on to London, still together. She had received a telegram which necessitated her going there on the same morning that Mr. van Schleeten left. She was to put up at the Grand Hotel Hermitage. On their arrival at Charing Cross she squeezed Mr. van Schleeten's hand in the straightforward, open-hearted manner that only a young American dares and invited him to the hotel the next day as her guest at dinner.

The dinner was delightful; above all when she insisted with the air of a princess that no one else but she would pay the bill. Mr. van Schleeten had been host to many young ladies; up to now he had never been their guest. It felt strangely stimulating, like some new sort of Dutch liqueur. He hastened to emphasize the fact that he could only conceive of allowing this under the condition that at the earliest possible moment she would join him in a little supper at the Savoy. She accepted, always with the same ingenuous air of a princess.

Toward the end of their dinner Mr. van Schleeten and his companion to their amazement saw at one of the tables in the dining room of the hotel no less a person than the young man from the train.

"Shouldn't we inform the police, Mrs. Langtrey?" said Mr. van Schleeten.

Mrs. Langtrey shook her beautiful head.

"I always love my neighbor when I have drunk champagne," she said.

Mr. van Schleeten decided that champagne and not Bordeaux should be served when they had their little supper at the Savoy.

This was Thursday, the eleventh of September. Mr. van Schleeten's business necessitated a hurried trip to Amsterdam which occupied the next three days. When he returned to London early Monday morning, the fifteenth, he received word that the Maharajah of Nasirabad would arrive in the metropolis that same day and, in order that His Highness might appear with suitable jewels as soon as possible, his presence was desired at the Grand Hotel Hermitage without delay.

Mr. van Schleeten felt a moment's surprise that His Highness and Mrs. Langtrey should have chosen the same hotel but quickly forgot it at the pleasant prospect of meeting her at the hotel and setting the date for their little supper which he now half thought might be transferred to a considerably more secluded spot than the Savoy, for instance to his own extremely quiet private apartment. He betook himself to the hotel without delay.

The manager himself received him and conducted him to the Maharajah's suite on the first floor. After a few minutes wait Mr. van Schleeten was ushered into the Maharajah's private apartment where he found himself in the presence of a brown-complexioned, dark-mustached young man, somewhat corpulently inclined, whom he took to be His Highness, a gray-bearded elderly Indian whose position in the household remained unknown to him, and an Englishman of military type with white mustache. It was the last-mentioned person who began to speak.

"You are Mr. van Schleeten of Amsterdam, the specialist in jewelry?"

"Yes."

"His Highness wishes to consult you regarding the alteration of some extremely valuable jewels. You understand, extremely valuable."

"Valuable!" interrupted the young Maharajah. "Morrel Sahib, how can you call them valuable! They are as unworthy of the white princesses as I myself. Perhaps they might be made worthy through the assistance of this man, in which case the reward and honor due him shall not be small."

"May I see the jewelry?" said Mr. van Schleeten, who found that this exchange of opinion spoke but poorly for the jewels and who kept thinking principally of Mrs. Langtrey.

At an order from Colonel Morrel, the doors to an adjoining room were opened and two black servants of severe and threatening countenance appeared bearing an iron and copper bound mahogany chest of goodly proportions. The black servants disappeared. Mr. van Schleeten was requested to look the other way and then heard several creaking, rasping sounds. Evidently the chest was unlocked through some complicated Open Sesame which they did not wish him to learn. Suppose the stones were no better than the Maharajah indicated, what then? Did they think it was the first time he had seen any jewels? Finally he was permitted to turn around. He did so and came near falling over with surprise.

Certainly, he had heard reports of the treasure stores of oriental princes and he himself had seen the majority of those belonging to European potentates, but this exceeded his wildest fancy. It was like a bit of the Thousand and One

Nights. It was a death blow to even his phlegmatic Dutch temperament. A torrent of varicolored stones, each and every one of which was worthy of being a crown jewel; a fountain of light; deep blue clusters of sapphires; ropes of pearls which curled in and out through the jewelled mass like dimly glowing gray serpents; emeralds flaming like tigers' eyes; a sprinkling of blood-red rubies over the whole, as though some faithless watchman had been beheaded on the chest and his blood had bespattered its contents—and everywhere, scattered among the other jewels, diamond after diamond, the cold glistening fire blazing like winter stars and Northern lights. All this sparkling color and self-born light seemed to hurl itself against Mr. van Schleeten like a volcanic eruption and almost took his breath away. Only after a while did he really notice the details, the rare stones varying in tint from the normal; black diamonds and diamonds of blue like the blue morning mists around the peaks of the Himalayas; emeralds of green melting into opal tones like the first blaze of an evening sky; rubies of red shading into blue as though to show their royal lineage—and last of all the gold mountings surrounding the gems. These were heavy, fantastic, at times even grotesque, but who would think of modernizing them! Mr. van Schleeten drew a deep breath and turning to the Maharajah stammered:

"And your Highness wishes me to alter them?"

"Of course," said Yussuf Khan with a stately mien. "Why else should I have you summoned here through Colonel

Morrel Sahib? He has informed me that you stand foremost in Europe among those skilled in handling precious stones. Although mine are of but little value and can hardly interest you, yet I beg you to make them as worthy as possible of the white princesses. Know, I am here in Europe seeking to win a Sahib princess, and let this thought be in your mind as your hands busy themselves with these stones. Your reward and the honor due you will be great."

Mr. van Schleeten, whose eyes were riveted on the chest and its contents like the eyes of a bird on a snake, thought of raising some further objections when Colonel Morrel forestalled him.

"This matter has been arranged in accordance with his Highness' wishes," he said briskly. "Will you undertake the work or shall we turn elsewhere? Let me know immediately."

Mr. van Schleeten remained silent a moment longer and then succeeded in answering:

"Of course—since his Highness wishes. But may I ask, in what way his Highness desires—"

"In whatever way you think best," interrupted the Colonel. "Decide that for yourself. It's your speciality, isn't it?"

As Mr. van Schleeten did not answer immediately he heard the Colonel mutter to himself: "What the deuce does it matter! One way is as good as another!"

Mr. van Schleeten began to understand how affairs stood, and then continued: "May I take his Highness' jewels to my workshop here in London, or—"

"You must work here," said the Colonel. "You will have a room at your disposal where you can bring all the appliances you need. Moreover, you must pardon the fact that his Highness' body-guard will keep watch outside the work room. It is not on your account, but to prevent attack from outside."

"I understand," murmured Mr. van Schleeten with gaze still fixed upon the chest and its contents. "And when shall I begin?"

"As soon as you can, as soon as you can," cried the Maharajah eagerly. "Preferably to-day."

"To-day, I fear, I must content myself with bringing the necessary appliances," said Mr. van Schleeten. "But I will start work to-morrow."

"Very well, to-morrow! And you promise to work as quickly as you can, do you not? The honor due you and your reward shall not be small, as truly as I am Yussuf Khan of Nasirabad, son of Ibrahim Khan."

"I will do my best, your Highness," said Mr. van Schleeten, bowing deeply as he started to leave. "If it is necessary I will work day and night."

The Maharajah was clapping his hands with delight as he reached the door. He saw the dusky servants come hurrying into the room in answer to a call from their master.

To his disappointment he learned when he inquired of the porter that Mrs. Langtrey had gone out. He wrote her a short note asking her if they could not meet before he started his work the next day in the Maharajah's apartment, and requested the porter to give it to her.

This was on the fifteenth of September. Tuesday, the sixteenth, brought forth a number of startling surprises for Mr. van Schleeten.

When he arrived at the Grand Hotel Hermitage about ten o'clock, he noticed immediately from the porter's manner that all was not as it should be. He had hardly entered the doorway when the porter rang for the manager and asked the latter to come to the office. Mr. van Schleeten bent over toward the porter with a confidential air.

"I left a little note with you yesterday," said he with a significant twinkle in his eye, as he stroked his yellowish-gray mustache.

It was a moment before the porter seemed able to recall the incident.

"Oh, yes!" he said. "Certainly. For the lady in 320-21. She has gone without leaving an answer."

"She has gone!"

Mr. van Schleeten's amazement and disappointment made him stress his words like an actor.

"She left this morning," said the porter, "about half-past seven. A telegram came for her shortly before."

"From America," murmured Mr. Schleeten, suddenly convinced that the troublesome suitor was putting in an appearance. How about his little supper now?

"No, from Paddington," said the porter. "I happened to notice the name of the place from the way the telegram was folded. Here is the manager."

Mr. van Schleeten, who at this moment saw the manager of the great hotel coming across the hall, was so stunned by the shock which the porter unwittingly had given him that he could neither think or speak. Therefore it took a while before he noticed that the manager was in as agitated a state of mind as he. He remained standing in front of Mr. van Schleeten and seemed to be at a loss for words. Finally it occurred to Mr. van Schleeten that it was rather singular that the manager had been called at all. He had nothing to do with him. He was on the point of asking what the trouble was when the manager seemed to come to a decision.

"Will you come upstairs with me to Colonel Morrel, Mr. van Schleeten?" he said. "You can speak with him yourself. That will be the best."

"What is the matter?" asked Mr. van Schleeten in astonishment.

"You must be discreet about what I am going to tell you, Mr. van Schleeten, for I suppose you must be informed of the matter. The Maharajah has disappeared and his apartment has been broken into during the night."

"Broken into!" stammered Mr. van Schleeten, for the moment forgetting Mrs. Langtrey and everything else but the marvelous jewels. "Were the jewels stolen?"

"No. Fortunately robbery was prevented at the last minute by a young man who is stopping here at the hotel. But the Maharajah has disappeared and God knows when we will see him again."

Mr. van Schleeten was at a loss how to reply. What sort of mysterious goings-on were these? Both Mrs. Langtrey and the Maharajah vanished! Had they run away together? Had he abducted her? Then, by all the infernal deities, he, Mr. van Schleeten, would have as little to do with the jewels as he would with the dirt in the street.

"When did he disappear?" he managed to ask.

"Last evening. He was enticed into some accursed place and has not been seen since. But in Heaven's name be discreet!"

Mr. van Schleeten breathed more freely.

Mr. van Schleeten's conversation with Colonel Morrel in the latter's room in his Highness' suite was short and summary. He found the Colonel pacing the floor from wall to wall like a newly caught tiger and looking hardly less bloodthirsty.

"What the deuce is the matter now?" was his cordial greeting.

"This is Mr. van Schleeten, Colonel," said the manager. "The jeweler, whom—"

"Jeweler, jeweler! When my black diamond, the De—"

Mr. van Schleeten began to feel offended. He had his own troubles at the moment, and found them sufficiently great to be spared being bothered with those of other people. He took a step forward toward the door.

"I will have somebody come and fetch my instruments," said he in an icy tone. "Allow me to tell you, Colonel, that I am not. . ."

"Fine! Fine! Hang it all, fine!" cried the Colonel, but then restrained himself as an idea struck him. "That is true—there is a possibility that those blind snoopers in there—" (obviously Colonel Morrel's pet name for the detectives) "will find his Highness!. . .Work whenever you please, my dear Mr. van Schleeten, absolutely when you please, then you will be doing my— his Highness a great favor. Good-bye!"

The Colonel rushed out of the room, and banged the door after him with a slam that sounded like the crashing of rocks. The manager turned to Mr. van Schleeten with an apologetic smile.

"The Colonel is a little excited," he said. "Don't be offended, Mr. van Schleeten. You know, an old soldier—it isn't exactly pleasant for him, just now."

"That is no reason why he should treat me as though I were a coachman who had driven in the wrong direction," said Mr. van Schleeten with a frown. "Each and every one of us has his own troubles."

"But, Mr. van Schleeten, you are a man of the world. Pay no attention to an old man's ill humor. Let me conduct you to the room which has been reserved for you."

Still somewhat resentful Mr. van Schleeten was shown to his work-room. The first view of the wondrous jewels was enough to make him forget both the Colonel and Mrs. Langtrey. He busied himself an hour admiring the stones one by one; two more, considering how he should 'change' the settings so they would appeal to the Maharajah's taste.

Then he ordered a light lunch with a small bottle of Château Lafitte, and afterwards settled down to work at about two o'clock. He kept at it until seven, scarcely noting how the time flew, he was so hypnotised by the stones; what he did note, however, when he put away his instruments, was that he would need an assistant if he was to finish the work within any time which could be considered reasonable, even without taking the Maharajah's nervous haste into consideration. At half-past seven he left the hotel.

The black body-guard still kept faithful, silent watch before the door to the work-room. Mr. van Schleeten spoke to them in English as he passed, but received no answer. Evidently they only understood their mother tongue.

Reaching the street, he at first moved half absent-mindedly through the bustling throngs. The September evening was a bit cool, with a touch of autumn in the air. It was only after a time that Mr. van Schleeten, whose head was filled with thoughts of the wonderful stones, realized he was hungry.

He went into a little French-Italian restaurant, whose doors he was passing, seated himself and chose several dishes à la carte and a small bottle of Kirman Cantenac. He was having some salad after the chicken when, looking up, he saw Mrs. Langtrey, alone and in walking costume, standing at his table. Mr. van Schleeten jumped up.

"You!" he cried. "You!"

"Yes, I—" she murmured. "Oh, I am so glad to meet you. May I sit down?"

Mr. van Schleeten pulled out a chair from the table with a speed as though he intended using it as a weapon, and assisted her in removing her coat. The little supper seemed to be beckoning, and in the rosy candlelight of his hopes he could already see himself offering her even further assistance. She sat down and absently toyed with the menu, which the French waiter had hastened to give her.

"To-night it is I who am host," said Mr. van Schleeten hastily. "Give me the wine list, waiter."

She nodded lightly and selected a couple of dishes. Mr. van Schleeten, who was carefully searching the champagne list, noticed that she gave her orders in French. He was a bit surprised and after the waiter had disappeared said:

"I thought you had never lived in France, Mrs. Langtrey."

"Lived in France?" she repeated after a moment. "No, why? Oh, because I spoke French! Doesn't every well-educated person do that?"

Mr. van Schleeten hastened to admit it.

It was while lingering over desert that they began to talk about him and what he was doing. Time, up till then, had been filled with her account of the reasons for her precipitate departure and with Mr. van Schleeten's expressions of sympathy at her recital. It was that troublesome suitor! Of course! The brutal egoist! (Mr. van Schleeten's verdict in general.) The inconsiderate fellow! Just simply to telegraph, "I am coming, await me," and then fancy that everything is all right, and the marriage can take place without further ado! Oh what contemptible types there are in this human comedy (this from Mr. van Schleeten). How bitter life is for an unfortunate woman without friends (Mrs. Langtrey). But how sweet when you have *one real* good friend (Mr. van Schleeten).

"Will you really be my friend?" she murmured.

Mr. van Schleeten declared himself ready to accept the part without reservations.

"A real genuine friend, nothing else?" she continued.

Mr. van Schleeten agreed to this also but not so eagerly, to be sure, as to the first program. However, he poured more champagne in her glass, relying on this yellow wine, and in case of need, on the future. This American was but a woman, and women, we know. . . Just a little besieging.

"How glad I am that I met you!" she whispered and, as though absentmindedly, let her slender fingers lightly touch Mr. van Schleeten's somewhat plump hand. "Think, how mere chance can help us, when we are in greatest need. That is, if it was mere chance."

Mr. van Schleeten declared himself fully convinced that it was Providence and sought to capture the slender fingers which quickly rescued themselves from his covetous grasp.

"Let us talk about yourself," she said, as though to break away from the former topic of conversation. "What are you doing now? Are you very busy?"

Mr. van Schleeten was seized with the desire to make himself interesting and to show his capabilities, the same desire which is the cause that he and all of us, thanks to our common ancestor, at the present moment do not dwell in Paradise. With an eloquence which evidently quite captivated her he described the commission which he had received from the Maharajah and became absolutely dramatic in his description of the jewels. Suddenly she interrupted him, her eyes sparkling:

"I *must* see them!" she cried. "I *love* jewels! More than anything else on earth."

"More than anything else on earth?" echoed Mr. van Schleeten disappointedly. "I am afraid it will be impossible, Mrs. Langtrey; I have been indiscreet through merely mentioning them to you."

"To me! Have you already forgotten you have promised to be my friend? If there is anything on earth that is worth more than diamonds it is true friendship. And to a real friend one should be able to relate his innermost secrets, isn't that so, Mr. van Schleeten?"

Mr. van Schleeten admitted she was right. But to show her the jewels. . .

"All right. Then we will say no more about it," she continued with a little tone of cool surprise in her voice which sent a shudder down Mr. van Schleeten's back. "You need not worry over your indiscretion. I don't tattle."

At the sound of that chilly voice, the rosy candlelight of Mr. van Schleeten's dreams for the future flickered as though struck by a draught of cold air. He hastily began in a stammering voice:

"Mrs. Langtrey. . . my dear friend. . . you see. . . what shall I say?. . . Wait, do not interrupt me! There *might* indeed be a possibility. . ."

Her eyes beamed warmly. "Let me hear!" she cried. "You *are* an angel!"

Mr. van Schleeten stroked his yellowish-gray mustache.

"As a matter of fact," he whispered, "I need someone to help me in my work. I found that out this afternoon. And if—that is to say, but you would have to put on men's clothes—and that?"

"Men's clothes! My, what fun! How you can think things out, my dear friend! You are an angel."

Mr. van Schleeten already began half-way to regret his words.

"But it will be difficult," he said hesitatingly. "You understand, if anyone should recognize you in the hotel then you as well as I would be irretrievably compromised."

"But if it were dark," she said, "no one would recognize me in disguise and under the electric lights. How late can you work there?"

"As late as I wish," Mr. van Schleeten admitted.

"Good, then you can be there at night, too!"

"I can," acknowledged Mr. van Schleeten.

"Then I will come at night," she cried with delight, glad to have solved a ticklish problem in such a simple way.

A shudder ran through Mr. van Schleeten. How would a little supper go, illuminated only by the glow from the wonderful jewels?

"You can come in the evening about ten o'clock," he said, "and I will notify the Colonel ahead of time that

I intend having someone to help me. At that time most of the hotel guests are either in bed or at the theater."

She clapped with delight and then squeezed his hand across the table.

"My, how jolly! It will be the jolliest experience of my life, and I have you to thank for it."

"But," stammered Mr. van Schleeten, who again regretted what he had done and who clung to this last straw, "there is a body-guard with drawn sabers before the door and. . ."

"That doesn't matter," cried Mrs. Langtrey "not in the least, when I know that I am with a real friend!"

Supper came to an end with Mrs. Langtrey, on her part, in a delightful frame of mind. But the hopes Mr. van Schleeten built on the champagne were not realized; in spite of that yellow and deceptive drink he was obliged to bid Mrs. Langtrey good-night at the door of a taxi (she had moved to a small family hotel, she said). A pressure from her soft yet firm hand and a glance through her veil promised delicious possibilities for the future, and on his way home Mr. van Schleeten succeeded in convincing himself that he was quite a dangerous fellow and that everything would go well. To-morrow night, in the Maharajah's room. . .

CHAPTER VIII

THE RETURN OF
YUSSUF KHAN

When the detectives finally had left and the Bowlby family under the guiding hand of Mrs. Bowlby had brought to a close their discussion of the attempted burglary and Mrs. Langtrey's disappearance, Allan began to think of his own private misfortune, but it would be untrue to say that he was especially affected by it. What was it he had whispered to himself a few days ago when he saw his native coast-line fade away? Forward, to meet adventure! Fate, *en garde*! Unquestionably he had found adventures; but Fate had also taken up his challenge, and had already delivered a decidedly perceptible counter thrust. If Mr. Mirzl had not been equally as eccentric as he was audacious, Allan would at this time have been minus both travelling bags and cash—and what could he have done, then? Telegraph home?—The mental picture of his creditors, undoubtedly by this time loudly crying out against him, made him hastily abandon carrying this thought to an end. At all events he was determined to avoid a repetition. Of course it could happen that Mr. Mirzl in his eccentricity might withdraw his sentence and send back the amount of the fine in the same way as he had the luggage, but while awaiting this it would be best to put the balance of the travelling funds beyond his reach. Consequently, on Wednesday Allan deposited his money in the hotel's banking department, to be surrendered only in return for checks or receipts signed by him. Two specimens of his own signature were given to the man in charge.

At seven o'clock the same evening Allan saw the old gentleman with the hawk-like nose, whom he now knew was the jewel specialist Mynheer van Schleeten, come toward the stairs from the Maharajah's apartment. He looked a bit excited. When the manager of the hotel a short time afterwards passed through the hall, Allan picked up his courage and approached him.

"May I speak to you a moment?"

The manager, who recognized Allan from the proceedings of the day before, nodded in a kindly manner. To be sure, this was the young man who had seen to it that not everything had gone absolutely wrong.

"You have no news of the Maharajah yet?"

The manager shook his head gloomily.

"No, I am sorry to say. You have kept a discreet silence, I hope?"

"Absolutely. I have not mentioned the matter to anyone excepting the Bowlbys. But there is another question I would like to ask. I just saw the old jeweler who was summoned by the Maharajah come down from the apartment. Is he working on the jewels although his Highness has disappeared?"

"Yes. He came this morning and as I did not know what to do about it, I took him up to Colonel Morrel—"

The director broke off and tried to suppress a laugh.

"I, myself, had the pleasure of meeting the Colonel yesterday morning," said Allan. "Mr. van Schleeten probably was requested to go to a certain warm place?"

"Something of the kind. But then the Colonel repented and begged—yes, *begged*—him to start on the work. Mr. van Schleeten has been working all day in the Maharajah's apartment."

"Do you not think he might fall into temptation, while alone?" said Allan. "He comes and goes when he pleases?"

"He? Why he himself is as rich as Croesus, and one of the best-known jewel-specialists in Europe! You might just as well suspect him of the burglary!"

"I am sorry," said Allan. "It is probably the burglary which has gone to my head. And then there is something else which by chance I happen to know."

"Yes?"

"I am accidently aware that Mr. van Schleeten is well acquainted with, or at least knows, Mrs. Langtrey, who disappeared yesterday morning."

"I have heard Mrs. Bowlby's insinuations about the lady in question. But the detectives shrugged their shoulders when they heard them and neither we nor they know anything to reflect discredit on her. And although you yourself saw her travelling on the same train as Mirzl, yet you did not venture to maintain that they knew each other. But of course they intend to keep an eye on her."

"All right," said Allan. "I merely wanted to tell you what I knew."

The manager bowed and went into his office.

Shortly afterwards Allan was witness to a scene which would have made him roar with laughter, if he had not understood the seriousness back of it all. The old Colonel came down the stairs and nervously rushed toward the office. In passing he cast an angry look at Allan. Evidently he was still far from convinced that it was not Allan himself who was the instigator of the whole affair. Before he reached the office, the manager came hurrying out again, his face blazing with excitement. At sight of the Colonel a slight cry escaped him. Allan noticed that he said something in a low voice to the old warrior. The Colonel stared at him fixedly, and then uttered a roar which made the people throughout the hall jump in their armchairs. The next moment he rushed up the stairs like a madman. Allan hurried over to the manager to ask what was the matter. Had they murdered the Maharajah?

"I'm sorry about Colonel Morrel!" said the manager. "The Lord only knows whether the whole hotel won't realize what's the matter after that last roar of his."

"What is it? Have they found his Highness' body?"

"It is not as bad as that—yet. But he has not been found

at all, and that is almost as bad."

"But the Colonel already knew that?"

"Yes, but Inspector McLowndes just telephoned—you know, the thin man who questioned you yesterday morning. His men have ferreted out the place you told them about."

"They have found the Fire-Eaters Club!"

"It seems that was not very difficult, only it had another name officially—The Franco-English Theatrical Friends, or something like that. The Fire-Eaters Club was a nickname among the members. A man by the name of Hardy is back of the whole society. Their papers are in order. Hardy had never heard of Mirzl or his confederates. A couple of days ago two gentlemen called on him, undoubtedly the ones you described; Stanton was one and the name of the other was Müller—evidently a German, as you thought. They were members of the club and engaged loges five and six for the evening, that was the whole affair and all that Hardy knew or wanted to know. The attendant did not know much more. How you managed to get out was an enigma to him, since he was the only one to let people in or out. About three o'clock he had answered a call from Number Five where he found the people from both Number Six and Number Five with the exception of you. He asked Müller about you, who replied that you were dancing and could remain as long as you liked. He, Stanton, and the two dark-complexioned gentlemen, who unfortunately were somewhat intoxicated, were going now. You understand, they had discovered your flight by this time and had become alarmed.

"The attendant helped carry down the Maharajah and the old court poet in the elevator; he seemed to have no suspicion as to their identity. Once down on the street they got into an automobile and he saw them drive away. He did not notice the number of the automobile, nor did he hear any address given. That is the whole story. You understand, therefore, that the Maharajah is in the clutches of those blackguards and of course you know what that will mean."

"Extortion?"

"That is the least, and we must admit, unfortunately, the most favorable result to expect. Extortion from me on account of the hotel and from the Colonel on account of his Highness—Oh, if I had never allowed those people to enter the hotel!"

The manager muttered something which Allan could not hear, but felt without doubt it was a rigorous oath. Allan had intended asking several other questions, but suddenly the manager hurried away without even bidding him good night.

Allan sat down in one of the chairs in the hall, ordered a whisky and soda and started thinking over the latest news. Parts of the affair were still hazy to him, thanks to the manager's abrupt way in closing the conversation. Hadn't the police rooted out more facts about the affairs of that club? Did Hardy know Mr. Stanton and Mr. Müller as members of the club? In that case he ought to know where they lived. Had the police tried to trace them through the automobile?

Allan went to bed without having seen the manager again or having received an answer to his questions. The Bowlbys had been invited out that evening, and a guard placed in their suite to prevent a repetition of Mr. Mirzl's visit.

The next day was as lacking in events as the two previous ones had been crowded with them. The Maharajah was and remained lost and not a word about a ransom from his kidnappers. Around seven in the evening Allan again saw the Colonel and felt a pang of pity for the old gentleman. He seemed so disturbed and nervous. Shortly afterwards, while he stood talking with Mr. Bowlby at the door to the dining-room, he saw the manager pass.

"If those villains would only write and set a price," he exclaimed. "Poor old Morrel will go crazy, if there is no news soon."

Allan took care to ask his questions this time. The manager shrugged his shoulders, and then the words came rattling out of his mouth in answer.

"Investigations! Of course the police are doing all they can, but we know what that amounts to! They are looking for the automobile. Hardy and the attendant have been examined half a dozen times to-day, and the list of club members has been scrutinized as though with the eyes of an Argus. Of course Stanton and Müller have moved a score of times since they became members, and not a soul knows where they live. The man who introduced them at the club, who strange to say is confoundedly exacting as to who should be admitted, was a French baron, de Citrac, or something."

"De Citrac!" Allan gave a start. "Do you remember the name, Mr. Bowlby? The man who flirted with Mrs. Langtrey in America, according to Mrs. Bowlby's story! Take my word for it, de Citrac is none other than his Majesty Mr. Mirzl himself."

The manager and Mr. Bowlby stared at him, and Mr. Bowlby brought forth a shrill, prolonged express-train whistle in testimony of his thoughts.

"By Jove! You are right, my young friend! Of course! You are right! I feel it in my bones."

The manager shrugged his shoulders.

"At all events, Hardy claims the man is rolling in riches and is owner of two or three castles in France. And even if it isn't true, it doesn't help matters much now, when something must be done quickly for poor Morrel's sake. It would be a blessing from heaven if the rascals would write and name their price, that's what I say, even though it sounds cowardly."

Mrs. Bowlby did not have as much sympathy for the Maharajah and his adviser as the manager when the subject came up for conversation at dinner.

"A pity about the Colonel! He might have taken better care of the Monster. *He*, at least, ought to have known what he is. When a person has had a hundred and fifty around him as a daily diet, he doesn't break himself of the habit immediately. You may say *what* you like, Mr. Cray, I *know* he was in the company of women there at that Place. Helen, my child, don't listen to what I am saying."

"No, Mamma!"

"And Langtrey's wife! Just think, those thick-headed detectives wouldn't even listen to what I told them about her! Innocent! Of course she is innocent because she wears skirts! I know men. It was she who informed the crooks that John invited Mr. Cray up to his room. Don't try to deny it, Mr. Cray."

"No, Mrs. Bowlby. You heard, did you not, that it was a Baron de Citrac who had introduced Mirzl's two assistants at the Fire-Eaters Club?"

"At that Place!"

"Yes, and do you not think it possible that de Citrac and Mirzl are one and the same person?"

"Why, of course! You are a genius, Mr. Cray. Why, of course! Then I am sorry for Mirzl. I really didn't think him half bad before, but if he has such taste—but do you know what *I* believe now, Mr. Cray?"

"No, Mrs. Bowlby."

"Simply that it is Langtrey's wife who has abducted the prince, and for herself! Everybody knows what sort of a man he is and she—Helen, my child, don't listen to what I am saying!"

"No, Mamma."

An idea occurred to Allan.

"Does anyone know whether the old jeweler has been at work here to-day too?"

Mr. Bowlby nodded.

"He came this morning as usual and worked here until half-past six. He talked with the manager—no one can speak a word to the Colonel now, and said that the work would take much more time than he had supposed. He asked permission to continue his work this evening and to bring a man from his office to help him. The manager talked it over with the Colonel and the Colonel gave his consent."

"I think I know in what form he gave it," said Allan.

After the dinner they gathered in the Bowlby apartment, where in addition to other comforts was some American whisky, highly appreciated by both Mr. and Mrs. Bowlby, though by the latter only in the quiet of her own apartment. Allan stayed until shortly before ten o'clock, when the Americans explained they wished to retire as they had been up late the night before. Allan was invited to remain and have a further nip alone, but he declined and said good-night.

On returning to the hall downstairs he stopped a moment to think what he should do. The immense hall was empty, excepting for a waiter and a couple of the hotel attendants. He decided to take a little evening walk through London's streets, and put on his overcoat, which he had left with the coat-boy.

Just as he was ready to go out, the revolving door began to turn and in came the old jeweler, and a plainly clad person. Evidently Mr. van Schleeten was keeping his word in regard to night work on the Maharajah's jewels. It was to be hoped that the Maharajah would have the opportunity of rewarding him for his zeal. Allan stepped aside to let Mr. van Schleeten and his assistant pass. He rather stared at them without thinking; Mr. van Schleeten gave him a couple of indignant looks in return. What reason did he really have for being angry with Allan? As a matter of fact, he had Allan to thank that he had the opportunity of working on the jewels. While passing them Allan gave a hasty glance at the assistant, who seemed to be a gawky fellow and ill at ease through the splendour of the great hotel; he didn't remove his cap which was drawn down tight over his head. Like a flash the thought went through Allan's mind that somewhere he had seen a pair of gray eyes, resembling those of the workman. Then he went on through the revolving door and down the broad marble steps.

He looked up at the façade of the hotel. In the Bowlby's suite light still appeared in a couple of the windows. The Maharajah's apartment was dark with the exception of one window, doubtless the one to the Colonel's room. While Allan was still looking, lights appeared in two other windows. So Mr. van Schleeten had arrived with his assistant. Allan was on the point of going on, when something peculiar happened.

For a moment a hand, with fingers outstretched, photographed itself on the window-pane where the light had just appeared. The fingers closed, opened and closed once again. Then two fingers were seen, spread widely apart;

thereupon the hand disappeared.

It had all happened with lightning speed. Allan, who still stood there, looking up, wondered whether he had seen correctly or whether he was the victim of an hallucination. No less a person than the manager of the hotel had borne testimony to the good name and reputation of Mr. van Schleeten. But how could this hand against the window-pane be explained other than as a signal to someone outside? And why signal anyone outside with the whole staff of servants of a large hotel at one's disposal? With all due respect for the manager. . .

Allan walked slowly along in front of the hotel, his eyebrows drawn together in a philosopher-like frown. Confused thoughts whirled through his head like snowflakes. Was Mirzl plotting with Mr. van Schleeten? It was not until half a minute or so after the mysterious hand had disappeared that he thought of something which should have been absolutely self-evident, namely: if any one signalled from the lighted windows in the hope of somebody outside seeing it, then that somebody must have been in the vicinity to note the signal. He began to look around him in the dimly lighted square where the hotel stood. A crowd of people were streaming by, although Monmouth Square was not one of the most frequented thoroughfares. The person evidently signalled had probably stood waiting in front of the hotel. Was there any mysterious sort of person stationed there? As far as Allan could see, there were only five or six automobiles. Well, there was nothing to prevent it being one of these, which someone. . .

Allan inwardly uttered a cry of triumph. Ha, ha! was that the little plan? Was Mr. van Schleeten a party to it? Or was he simply a marionette, operated by the thread through which he most readily responded? Mr. Bowlby had heard of and discussed his leanings toward the weaker sex. Was it with the knowledge of this fact, and with malice aforethought, that Mrs. Langtrey had been so gracious to him on the express-train and had become so inflamed at Allan who threatened to disturb their tête-a-tête? And *was* it conceivable that this might be the reason why the assistant, clad in workman's clothes, had gray eyes which seemed so familiar to him? A swarm of thoughts, all radiating from this last idea as starting point, buzzed through Allan's head. And after he had quickly reached the conclusion that he was right, which tickled both his egotism and his desire for revenge, there remained but one question: what should he do?

He walked back and forth on the sidewalk looking, now at the lighted window where a hand was no longer seen, now at the people who passed by, among whom he tried to discover some accomplice. The manager? Should he go to him? He would surely only be laughed at. The manager had expressed his faith in Mr. van Schleeten too firmly for him to change his opinion through a mere whimsical idea held by a young fellow like Allan—even admitting that Allan had already hit on some rather happy conclusions. Perhaps after all it was but a whimsical idea about it not being a workman who had gone upstairs with Mr. van Schleeten, about the signal and all the rest. What could the authorities really do to Mr. van Schleeten *if* Allan was right? Why, there was the guard in front of his door.

A new thought struck Allan. What awakened it was nothing less than the sight of Colonel Morrel's window, where the light was still burning.

The Colonel! *He* left nothing to be desired in the way of readiness to suspect anybody and most likely Allan above all others!. . .

But without wasting time deliberating further as to whether some other way were better suited, or how this one would turn out, Allan rushed up the steps to the hotel and then on to the Maharajah's suite. He saw the black body-guard, keeping watch in the corridor, in front of the rooms engaged by their ruler. The Colonel's room was at the end of the corridor and in front of it stood a man in livery carrying a syphon and a bottle of whisky on a tray; he stood with his fist still raised to the door as though he had just knocked. The Colonel evidently wished to drown his troubles in a little evening's inebriation. Just as the man opened the door, Allan came up.

"I must speak to the Colonel," he cried and seized the man's arm.

The man in livery looked at him with utter indifference.

"The Colonel does not receive at this time of day," said he, and tried to free himself from Allan's grip. But Allan clung to him as though to a life-buoy. Now once in the boat, devil take it, but he would be rowed ashore.

"It will be at your own risk, if you refuse to announce me. Do you hear, at your own risk! My name is Allan Kragh, the Colonel knows who I am. Do you hear?"

Allan did not have a chance to finish. Colonel Morrel, deathly pale from his excited condition, suddenly appeared in the doorway. It was unmistakable that the whisky the servant was bringing him was not the first he had seen that day. He had difficulty in preserving his military bearing and his eyes, which hurled forth dagger-like glances, seemed to have even more difficulty in sighting their mark correctly.

When he caught sight of Allan he roared like a tiger.

"You! What in thunder are you doing here? Have you succeeded in stealing the jewels or have your comrades informed you what they demand for the Maharajah?"

Allan came straight to the point.

"Colonel Morrel, I shan't bother to answer your accusations. It may perhaps interest you to know that plans have evidently been laid to steal the jewels this very night, if so, you know it now. Good evening!"

The Colonel was over the threshold with a bound and seized Allan by the arm.

"Good evening! What in thunder do you mean? Do you intend to steal the jewels to-night and then come here and tell me about it beforehand? Lord help me, if you—"

Allan gave the old fighter a look which really made him let go of Allan's arm and stop in the midst of what he was saying. He stared about for a moment and then looked at Allan.

"What in thunder did you say?" he muttered indistinctly.

"What I said, Colonel Morrel, was that I think they have planned an attempt to steal the jewels to-night. Do you hear, *to-night*? Perhaps at this very moment, perhaps within an hour. I do not know it absolutely, but I believe it. Does it interest you enough to send back that whisky?"

The Colonel angrily drew himself up, but then he lowered his eyes again.

"Take it away, John," said he. "No more this evening. Come in, young man."

He showed the way to his room, then went to the bathroom and sponged his forehead a couple of times. Thereupon he returned to Allan.

"Will you smoke?" said he. "No? Tell me what you think you know."

Allan went over as slowly and explicitly as he could the few facts he had in support of his theory. The Colonel listened with knitted brow. A couple of times his eyes showed that he had difficulty in keeping all his wits about him. Allan continued repeating his story, until he thought he made it perfectly clear. When he told the Colonel that was all, the latter shook his head.

"I do not want to insult you," said he. "I have certainly done so enough in the past. But—isn't the evidence in favor of your theory rather slight in proportion to the theory itself?"

"That is perfectly true. But how do you explain

the hand?"

"Just chance. And if your theory were correct, what could a woman do? Van Schleeten is no child. And how could she get away with her booty?"

"That I cannot say. But how do you account for van Schleeten's zeal in his work, and that, too, at this time of night?"

"Through the special request of his Highness. In the beginning he expressed his willingness to work nights, and that was long before the first attempt at robbery."

Allan bowed his head and became thoughtful. The Colonel was right. His theory was fantastic, but at all events—He turned to the old fighter.

"Colonel Morrel!" said he, "I desire nothing else but that you give me a simple proof. You understand that the matter really does not concern me at all. But let us go to the room where van Schleeten is working, and see if everything is all right. Or you go in alone! You can do that without causing the least comment."

The Colonel pondered. He shrugged his shoulders a couple of times and Allan thought he had already failed, when the Colonel suddenly rose from his chair.

"All right!" said he. "It would be unpardonable of me not to do that in simple fairness to you. I will go at once. You may follow me, if you wish, so that you can see into the room. I would prefer not taking you in with me, for reasons you can well understand."

They left the Colonel's room with punctilious observation of the rules of courtesy on both sides—Allan insisting the older gentleman precede him and the Colonel insisting his guest should have this honor. At last it was Allan who won through his polite Swedish stubbornness. After a few steps across the heavy oriental rug in the corridor they had reached the door to the room of the Maharajah's suite which had been assigned to Mr. van Schleeten. The black body-guard saluted with their curved yataghans at sight of the Colonel. He spoke a few words to them in a croaking sort of dialect.

"I asked them whether they had heard anything suspicious," the Colonel explained, turning to Allan.

"Had they?" asked Allan.

"No, but let us make our own investigations anyway."

He took hold of the door knob. The door was bolted. Before Allan could prevent it he had raised his hand and knocked.

"Colonel Morrel!" Allan whispered, "what are you doing? If it should be—"

He did not have time to finish his remark. There had been no reply to the knock from inside, and all at once the rage, born of whisky, and which had but slumbered in the Colonel, burst into full blaze. He uttered a roar, grabbed a saber from one of the black soldiers and before Allan realized what was happening had cleaved the panel of the door with a single blow, which thundered through the corridor like a cannon shot. Two more blows and then he threw himself against the door with all his strength. It gave way with a crash. The Colonel rushed in with Allan at his heels and the black soldiers streaming along behind them. They caught a glimpse of a strange figure before it disappeared to the accompaniment of six revolver shots fired in quick succession by the Colonel.

The window stood open and at the moment they came into the room, they caught a momentary glimpse above the window ledge of a plainly clad person, or rather, the head of that person, wearing a gray cap. It disappeared outside the window just as they crossed the threshold, followed by the six shots from the Colonel's revolver; and Allan hardly had time to wonder how the head could disappear there before he reached the window and found the solution to the problem. A slender rope-ladder hung down the side of the hotel reaching to the sidewalk; the person whom they had seen disappear had already arrived at the bottom, and just as Allan and Colonel Morrel reached the window, came the most surprising in that series of events which were following each other in lightning-like succession. The fugitive, who must have glided down the rope-ladder with the suppleness of a snake and who by this time must have been perfectly aware of the seriousness of the situation, found time to make a quick movement of the hand—it was a match being lighted. Just as Allan put his leg over the window-ledge to slide down the rope-ladder, it flamed up from one end to the other; it must have been saturated ahead of time with some inflammable preparation. Allan had barely time to pull himself back from the window-ledge before the flames reached the top with a hiss. In impotent rage the Colonel hurled his empty revolver after the escaping figure. He missed his mark, and in a moment the fugitive was in a shining black automobile, which seemed to spring up from nowhere.

Allan and the Colonel turned to each other and their eyes spoke the same words: Too late! and then they both caught sight of something which drew their thoughts in another direction.

And that something was Mynheer Jan van Schleeten, the celebrated specialist in jewels, known throughout Europe, who, on a couch in the corner of the room, had raised himself on his elbow and was staring about him with vacant eyes and wide-open mouth. At his side stood a workbench and a mahogany chest filled to overflowing with glittering precious stones. And the first words Mr. van Schleeten said were:

"She. Where is she?"

Now it was Allan who was master of the situation. With two steps he was at Mr. van Schleeten's side, took from this gentleman's breast a handkerchief which was wringing wet, and held it up to the Colonel:

"Do you see, Colonel Morrel, what a weak woman can do? Enough chloroform for a horse! Now we must see whether or not we have come in time. Mr. van Schleeten, get up and help us, and remember that your name and your honor are at stake!"

The old Dutchman raised himself from the couch,

staggering like a person dead drunk. The Colonel had immediately sunk into a state of lethargy after the flight of the culprit and was staring helplessly about him. It was Allan who had to look after everything.

"Will you order some coffee brought up here, Colonel Morrel!" he cried. "You see the condition Mr. van Schleeten is in! Strong coffee is the only thing that can straighten him out."

The Colonel mumbled a few words to one of the black body-guard, who at once rushed away. A minute later, with the help of Allan, Mr. van Schleeten gulped down a cup of steaming, shining black coffee. The first thing he did thereafter was to draw himself up and stare at Allan.

"I know you," he said in a thick voice, "you are—you are a criminal."

"Hold your tongue, man," yelled the Colonel, suddenly awakening from his stupor. "You can thank your lucky stars that this young man is here! Otherwise you would be sitting between four prison walls in the morning!"

Mr. van Schleeten stared at him with dull eyes.

"But I saw him," he muttered, "saw him at a railroad station—where was it?—why, of course—at the st-station in Co-Cologne, and he was under ar-arrest. It is h-he who has. . ."

"Drink the rest of your coffee and shut up!" roared the Colonel. "And then go to the chest and see what pieces are missing!"

It took a while before Mr. van Schleeten succeeded in

complying with these three requests. The examination of the mahogany chest took a long time; a time during which Allan went downstairs and had the startled night porter telephone to the police. But when he came up stairs again, he had the satisfaction of seeing Colonel Morrel rush to meet him. The Colonel grasped both his hands and seemed to rather want to kiss him.

"The settings were too large and cumbersome, and she was in too much of a hurry!" he shouted. "It is possible that one of the diadems is missing, but that is all, that cursed Dutchman swears! It was that sly little devil of an adventuress who trapped him, and would have succeeded if you had not—"

Allan, with true Swedish embarrassment and shyness, tried to interrupt him. It took some time before he got to bed that night; partly because they all had to be examined by the detective, Inspector McLowndes, who had arrived on the scene (after the examination Mr. van Schleeten was permitted to go home accompanied by a detective); partly because Colonel Morrel refused to retire before he had increased his inebriety of earlier in the day by consuming a bottle of champagne with Allan. With the bottle emptied he declared that, without any exception, he had never before met a person on whose brow all good qualities were so distinctly and harmoniously united as on Allan's.

* * *

Allan, while dressing, was interrupted at ten o'clock the next morning by Mr. Bowlby, who unceremoniously opened the door to his room. What he came to relate was nothing less than that Yussuf Khan and the venerable Ali had been found that same morning at half-past six in Victoria Park in the East End, in a complete state of unconsciousness, and each embellished with a label reading: 'To be forwarded to the Grand Hotel Hermitage.'

Allan had not asked all the questions he wanted—in fact, Mr. Bowlby was acquainted with hardly more than the main fact, which he had heard from the manager—and he himself had been unable to relate more than an outline of his experiences of the night before, when he received a new shock. Still accompanied by Mr. Bowlby, he went down to the hotel's banking department for the purpose of drawing a few pound of the money he had on deposit.

The young man at the desk stared at him for a moment, and then in a half-frightened, half-suspicious manner, asked him how could he have forgotten, that he had already been there an hour before and had then withdrawn his entire balance.

CHAPTER IX

'The Morning After' for Prince And Poet

Allan stared at Mr. Bowlby and Mr. Bowlby at Allan. Then Mr. Bowlby let out a whistle that cut like a sword as it echoed throughout the hotel, a whistle as though from an express locomotive shrieking: *Life in danger, all brakes on hard, stop short!*

"Mirzl again, by Jove!"

At last a sound came from Allan's throat as he turned to the clerk.

"May I speak to your manager?"

"For the moment I am alone in charge, sir, but if you like I will ring for the manager of the hotel. It looks as if something were wrong, although I can't understand what it is."

"Thanks, please call him."

Three minutes later, the manager came hurrying into the office. Even at a distance it was evident that he was not in the best of humor, and the remark he made to Mr. Bowlby as he entered the door, at once revealed the cause.

"The Lord only knows why I ever asked you to move out of your suite, Mr. Bowlby!"

"Is there anything new?"

"New! Nothing more nor less than four score reporters who have been after me during the morning. Finding the Maharajah in the East End and in such a condition was all over Fleet Street in ten minutes. Those idiotic bobbies who ran across him, of course didn't know enough to hold their tongues. . . And with a hole in the floor which has to be repaired and with a door the Colonel hacked into more pieces than George Washington chopped the cherry tree! It's a fine thing to have guests of quality, eh?"

"You have had another guest of quality here this morning, too, without knowing it," said Mr. Bowlby. "Listen!"

He told what had happened to Allan. The manager stared at him as though he were a ghost. At last he stammered:

"Well. . . what do you mean? Who has been here?"

"Mirzl! You know he took half of my young friend's money the first time he found himself thwarted. How he found out the balance was deposited here, I can't understand."

"Perhaps that is not so difficult to explain," Allan remarked and then turned to the young man at the desk. "You say that I was here an hour ago and withdrew what I had on deposit. Give us the particulars."

The young man cast a frightened glance at the manager and began:

"It was just as I opened up. A gentleman who looked exactly like you, sir, came in and turning to me said, 'How much was it that I deposited with you?' 'What name, sir,' said I, as a matter of form, although I had immediately recognized you, sir. 'I had better spell it for you,' said he, and smiled. 'Allan K-r-a-g-h. A difficult name to pronounce.' 'All right, sir,' said I and referred to my books. 'You have on deposit a little more than five thousand Swedish crowns, three hundred English pounds.' 'All right, let me have them,' said he. 'Give me a receipt—blank, and I will sign it.' 'Have you the receipt which I gave you when you deposited the money, sir?' I asked. He looked in his pockets. 'Why, how stupid! I must have left it in my other suit of clothes. But if I sign for the money now, I can give you the receipt a little later.' 'All right, sir,' said I, for I had no suspicion that it could be any one else than Mr. Kragh and the handwriting was. . ."

"To the deuce with it all!" shrieked the manager. "Soon I will be as crazy as the Colonel. Reporters, burglars, thieves of all sorts, black princes who are found in the parks at six o'clock in the morning—it is enough to make one go mad! From this day on people will have to undergo examination by the police before they can poke their noses inside the door of my hotel!"

Mr. Bowlby tried to calm him down.

"You should be a little more grateful to my young friend from Sweden. He has twice prevented the Maharajah being robbed. . ."

"Then for heaven's sake he should prevent himself being robbed, too!" cried the manager. "Grateful! Of course I am grateful. How much was it in English money?"

"Five thousand four hundred in Swedish, three hundred English pounds," said Allan briefly. "Don't bother about it. But I will have to ask you for a few days' grace in paying my bill as Mr. Mirzl has appropriated all my funds."

The manager grasped his hand and shook it.

"There, there!" the manager exclaimed. "Don't be angry. Don't misunderstand me. Of course the hotel is responsible for the money you deposited. But in this case the circumstances are such that I cannot settle the matter myself offhand. Don't misunderstand me. If you had been having the Colonel after you for three days and a swarm of reporters buzzing around your ears all the morning—Lord, there comes the Colonel! What's the matter now? What sort of crime has been committed in the hotel now?"

The look on the Colonel's face was not so sunny but what the manager might have good reasons for being suspicious. However, the suspicions proved to be unfounded.

"I heard you were here," he cried to the manager. "In mercy's name why don't you kick out this pack of scandalmongers? They have been chasing after me like dogs after a fox. 'Is it true that the Maharajah was found as good as dead in the parks? Is it true that they attempted to get away with his jewelry at the same time they tried to make away with him? What does the Maharajah think of London? What is your opinion about this peculiar assault on him?'

'*Gentlemen*,' I shouted at them, 'I am of the firm opinion that you are a lot of cursed vampires, and if you don't get out on the spot I will try to express myself more plainly with a six-shooter. The Maharajah thinks London would be a charming city, if there were no Londoners, and to avoid seeing them as much as possible, his Highness has formed the habit of taking an early morning walk through the parks in the East End where to-day he was unfortunately overcome by an attack of faintness, which gave rise to a thousand idiotic reports, only believed by those people who are stupid enough to read newspapers that have been written by greater idiots than themselves; and if you are not satisfied with this explanation, gentlemen, then. . .'"

The Colonel's voice trembled with excitement, but without causing his audience any difficulty in completing his unfinished sentence. Mr. Bowlby wiped his eyes and said:

"You ought to be Minister of Foreign Affairs, Colonel, then there would be more dispatch with diplomatic proceedings! Have you seen Mr. van Schleeten to-day?"

"Schleeten! I have had more than enough of that whole crowd. He will probably put in an appearance later in the day, and then he will be told so plainly. I happened to think of something this morning. Who can say Schleeten did not have a hand in the matter? I think it was a plot, and I shall ring up the detectives about it."

"But, Colonel, one of the oldest and most highly respected jewelers. . ."

"Who allows himself to be duped by some cursed little adventuress in trousers. It *was* a conspiracy, you can be sure of that, Bowlby."

"She probably does not go around in trousers regularly, Colonel. And how do you explain the chloroform? You yourself saw him lying there unconscious."

"As if that did not prove the *conspiracy*. Haven't we heard a thousand times how people stage mock-burglaries? I did not happen to think of that before. I will telephone to the detectives about it at once. Good morning, my young friend. How are you?"

It was not until now that he seemed aware of Allan's presence.

"Thank you, Colonel," said Allan, "as well as can be expected of a person who has just been robbed of all his ready money."

"Of all your ready money! She and Schleeten were back of it!"

"I do not doubt that Mr. van Schleeten is equally willing to declare that it was she and I who arranged the affair last night. No, it was another friend of hers whom you have also become acquainted with lately—Mr. Benjamin Mirzl."

The Colonel listened with staring eyes to Allan's story, twirled his white mustache and uttered a few pointed remarks concerning his opinion of Mrs. Langtrey and Mr. Mirzl:

"How long are those blind snoopers going to let these gentry remain at large? I am beginning to believe that Mirzl is the devil himself!"

The manager interrupted him:

"How about his Highness, Colonel?"

The Colonel's brow became clouded. "Both he and the other beauty are still dead drunk. The Lord only knows what those scoundrels poured into them. The doctor and nurses have been working an hour with massage and injections and electricity, and have stood them on their heads and on their feet, without producing the faintest sound from them. The doctor thinks it is ether or morphine or both."

"Isn't it rather queer, Colonel," Allan ventured to remark, "that the kidnappers let them go? And without trying to exact any money from them! On the very night, too, that their other plan miscarried!"

"I don't care a snap about that," answered the Colonel heartily. "But as soon as they can put their noses outside the door again, off they go to India. I'll see to that! I will call on the Home Secretary for India this afternoon and explain the matter to him privately. And then his Highness can protest until he is blue in the face, but there will be no further European visit for him and no courting of beautiful white princesses."

The manager of the great hotel looked up with an expression of the most profound gratitude and took his leave, after giving the young man in the banking department orders to pay Allan whatever money he might need at the moment. Allan turned to the Colonel.

"May anyone see the patients, Colonel?"

"Not yet, my young friend. I think I will go up and look after them now for a while. We will meet again later."

He rushed away. Mr. Bowlby looked at his watch.

"Almost time to have a bite to eat," he said. "Let us go and see what Susan and Helen are planning to do."

They found Mrs. Bowlby and Miss Helen in the Bowlby's sitting-room. Mrs. Bowlby wore a purple dress, which made her look strikingly like a Brazilian cockatoo.

"Well, at last!" she cried. "Where have you been keeping yourself so long, John? Helen and I have nearly perished from curiosity. What has happened? Is it true that the Monster was found on the street half dead from his carouse? The servants say so. And what about that old gray-haired reprobate? Do tell me all about it, John! And is it a fact that the third member of that estimable company during an attack of delirium last night cut down the body-guard and knocked big holes in the floor and walls? Do tell me all about it, John!"

"As soon as you will let me, my dear Susan. The Maharajah—"

"It is true, of course! Half dead from dissipation! Helen, you should not listen to this, my child; but it may be useful for you to know what men can do. And the Colonel, John?"

"Dear Susan, let me first say just a couple of words about the Maharajah."

"You are going to defend him, of course."

"The Maharajah, Susan dear, was found early to-day in a park in the East End, drugged."

"With drink!"

"Drugged with ether or morphine by those scoundrels who kidnapped him and the old court poet."

"That is what they say, ha, ha!"

"That is not what they say, since the doctor has not yet succeeded in bringing either the Maharajah or old Ali back to consciousness."

"Ha, ha, John, you are really too unsophisticated!"

"All right, but you asked about the Colonel."

"Who had an attack of delirium last night. That's what the servants say. I *will* admit that the poor prince is not surrounded by shining examples. We should do him that much justice. When he is lured into terrible Places by an old reprobate of his own religion, and sees a white-haired hypocrite, who calls himself a Christian, get dead drunk, then it is easy to understand that a person of weak character may be led into temptation. And then not having a wife's support, too."

"He has a hundred and fifty of them, my dear Susan."

"I do not call those wives, John, as you well know."

"You have done so before, my dear Susan."

"Because I wished to protect my little Helen's ears. She has to hear enough, anyway, poor child."

Mrs. Bowlby changed the topic of conversation.

"How about the Colonel, John? Has he been taken to the hospital?"

"Not yet, my dear Susan. I just left him a moment ago. He was going up to take a look at his charges. He was a bit excited after his conversation with thirty or forty reporters. Otherwise he was all right. And if you will allow Mr. Cray to talk in anywhere near peace, you will find out how the whole thing hangs together with the Colonel's delirium. You have faith in Mr. Cray."

"As much faith as I can have in a man, John, after twenty years of married life."

"Dear Susan, now don't be angry at me because I have robbed you of your illusions about the Maharajah and the other two. Begin your story, Mr. Cray!"

Allan repeated his account of what had happened the night before. Mrs. Bowlby listened almost calmly until he reached the scene which met their eyes when the Colonel and he entered van Schleeten's work-room. Then she let out a yell worthy of the baseball-playing American nation.

"He too! A swindler! The old robber! So the jewels have been stolen?"

"Not yet, Mrs. Bowlby. The Colonel and I arrived at just the right second to prevent it, and I am certain it was the Colonel's sword attack on the door which frightened the thief away."

"The thief? You mean his accomplice!"

"You take the same viewpoint as the Colonel, when you say that, Mrs. Bowlby. But if you will permit my saying so, it is not correct. It was an adventuress who duped Mr. van Schleeten."

There was a short circuit in the network of Mrs. Bowlby's brain.

"An *adventuress*! Why, you said it was a person in man's clothes who went upstairs with him?"

"True, still it was an adventuress at all events, Mrs. Bowlby, but dressed as a man."

"In trousers! Why, I would rather. . . Now you see, Helen, to what lengths women will go, when they once get started. A hundred times worse than the men. Who was it, Mr. Cray? Do they know who it was? Was it a Hollander?"

"No, an American. Draw a deep breath, before I mention her name."

"You do not mean. . .?"

"Yes, exactly that. Mrs. Langtrey!"

Mrs. Bowlby had doubtlessly heeded his advice concerning the deep breath, for she let out a cry that pierced him through and through.

"Then I was right, Mr. Cray?"

"It seems so, Mrs. Bowlby."

"Think of that dissipated old rascal, letting himself be led astray by a woman—Helen, my child, don't listen to what I am saying—a woman in trousers!"

"He got his punishment, Mrs. Bowlby. She chloroformed him and would have stolen all the jewels, if we had not come in time. She succeeded in escaping, but she had to leave the jewels behind her. It was lucky for her that the Colonel's hand shook. He fired six shots through the window. But I must admit that I admire her for her coolness in setting fire to the rope-ladder."

"You should never admire anything that is bad, Mr.

Cray. And she was cheated out of the jewels?"

"Yes, and as a reward for what I did, Mr. Mirzl has relieved me to-day of the balance of my money."

"'Pon my soul, now, what do you mean?"

Allan related what had happened in the hotel's banking department. Mrs. Bowlby listened to him with eyes wide-open. When he had finished, she drew a deep breath and said:

"I must admit that this Mirzl. . . Just think of his having fallen into the clutches of Langtrey's wife. I am sure she is the one who led him astray just as she did that old thief of a jeweler."

"Do you think she chloroformed him, Mrs. Bowlby?"

"A woman does not need chloroform for such things. I must say that I almost admire that Mirzl anyway."

"You should never admire anything that is ba—"

"No impertinence, young man, demmit. It is the second time you have succeeded in blocking his game. Do you think that will put an end to his efforts?"

"It seems improbable. But as soon as the Maharajah gets well—puts his nose outside the door again, as the Colonel so politely expresses it, he will be taken back to India. The Colonel has given his oath on that. And by that time I expect Mirzl will have lost his chance."

After lunch Allan strolled up to the first floor. The black body-guard stopped him, but with a grin of recognition. A curtain hung in front of the door, which the Colonel had hacked down. Allan sought to make himself understood by the black soldiers, but they answered simply with a single word, which Allan finally decided meant *Colonel*. The Colonel had evidently forbidden anyone being admitted.

"Let me speak to the Colonel," said he.

They shook their heads and were making some unintelligible remark, when the door opened a little and a pale turbaned head showed itself. It was the venerable Ali.

"Most honorable poet!" Allan cried out. "Let me come in and press your hand. How are you? Do you not remember me from the House of a Thousand Joys, also called the Fire-Eaters Club?"

The old court poet stroked his brow.

"The House of a Thousand Joys was a masked entrance to the Palace of Pain," said he. "It seems to me now that I remember you, young man. Is it of you they spoke to us? Was it you who succeeded in escaping from those sons of Sheitan and prevented them stealing the jewels of my disciple?"

"It was my own unworthy self," said Allan.

"Enter then, that blessings may be showered on you! Not so much by me—for what are precious stones other than so many tinted pebbles?—but by my disciple, whose heart in its youthful folly is filled with this world's phantom images, bright and many-colored, of which such jewels are but symbols. By the Prophet, how my head aches! Not since Jamshyd and Kaikobad has there been such deep drinking. May the great Judge forgive me! Enter!"

Allan passed through a lane of drawn swords. Once

inside, he found the person around whom so may intrigues had been spun. He was lying stretched out on a couch, in the same position as when Allan had last seen him at the Fire-Eater's Club, but he seemed to have a much weaker and less happy smile on his face than then. Through the half-open door to an inner room he caught glimpses of a nurse. As Allan entered Yussuf Khan raised both hands in greeting.

"You are more than a thousand times welcome!" said he in a faint voice. "Forgive me for not rising, noblest sahib! It has been forbidden me. Tell me what you desire as reward for your services to me! Don't hesitate to tell me!"

"Let us speak of that some other time," said Allan. "It was more by chance than through my efforts that the robbers were unsuccessful. Instead, let me hear what experiences your Highness and this most worthy of poets have had since we last met."

The venerable Ali sank down in a chair after he had drawn one forward for Allan.

"Be seated," said he. "Like my disciple, I am exhausted from the treatment we suffered from the sons of Sheitan. According to what Colonel Morrel Sahib imparted to me when I reawakened here, I have forever lost my good name and reputation. With right did the Divine Tentmaker say of himself:

> *Indeed the Idols I have loved so long*
> *Have done my credit in this World much wrong:*
> *Have drown'd my Glory in a shallow Cup,*
> *And sold my reputation for a Song.*

The same was said of me by Colonel Morrel Sahib, though not in such melodious words as were used by the divine Omar. I know scarcely anything about what I went through, my young friend, and still less about my disciple's experiences. From the time I saw him out stretched on the couch in the House of Joys, a mild and friendly smile playing on his lips, I have not seen him again until to-day, in this room, when I opened my eyes, with lids as heavy as lead. I was surrounded by young women clad in white, who were kneading me over and over, like misers pawing their gold, and almost more eagerly. There was also in the room a *hakim*—physician—all in white, and my disciple and Colonel Morrel Sahib, who at once told me I ought to be beheaded and then hung outside the walls of Nasirabad as a mild punishment for my evil deeds, which he said were so bad that the language of the sahibs lacked words to describe them."

"Where is Colonel Morrel now?" Allan succeeded in asking. He could well imagine the Colonel's eloquence.

"Colonel Morrel Sahib has gone to consult the Home Secretary for India on matters, the importance of which he intimated to us. My disciple and I, who have lost our good name and reputation in this city, which never before heard of such behavior, are to be taken home as quietly and discreetly as possible. That is what Colonel Morrel Sahib is trying to obtain for us as a special act of grace from the Home Secretary for India, who had intended to drive us from the country shorn of our turbans and with dirt on our heads."

"But did you remember nothing about the Fire-Eaters Club until to-day?" Allan asked. "That was three days ago now!"

"My young friend," said the venerable poet, "I am a true believer in the Prophet, and have always tried to keep myself untainted by such false doctrines as a belief in Nirvana and similar inventions of an erring imagination. But when I think back to the time you just mentioned, I have a lamentable inclination to believe that these teachers of false doctrines are not entirely wrong, so completely was my consciousness blotted out during that time, which you say lasted three days. And my disciple, whom I have questioned concerning his feelings, says the same in regard to himself."

"That is true," feebly came Yussuf Khan's voice from the sofa. "What my teacher says is as true as the Koran. I remember nothing but a great darkness in which I seemed to float as on a restless sea, tormented by ugly dreams. Suddenly someone grasped at my soul, as one grasps at a drowning man, and when I raised my head above the black waters I found myself in this room surrounded by nurses all in white and a white-clad *hakim*. The scoundrels who lured us into the House of Joys, and afterwards kidnapped us, did not succeed in stealing my jewels, thanks to you, but instead they stole three days of my life."

"My disciple speaks well," said the venerable Ali admiringly. "If, as Colonel Morrel Sahib declares, I have set him such a bad example that this whole city is indignant over my actions and would like to see me drawn and quartered, yet I notice that I have to some extent succeeded in cultivating his sense of poetry and eloquence. To Allah—let his name be ever praised—is due the honor for this. Now I remember something which I had forgotten before. While my soul lay enveloped in darkness like in a prison with walls of never ending thickness, suddenly there filtered into it, through the walls, a little ray of light. Like in a dream and as though peering through a dense mist, I remember I was lying outstretched on a couch, whether undressed or not I do not know. Not far from me on another couch, it seemed to me, was my disciple. Just as I became conscious of this impression, I thought I saw a man, who had stood leaning over me, leave my couch and go to that of my disciple's, where he bent over him with a malicious grin, such as the idols in the temples of the unfaithful bear upon their faces. And, strangely enough, I thought I became aware of a woman just beside him. Still, what is there strange in this? Where the wicked gather, there women too will be found in plenty, says the proverb, and the Koran (may it be forever praised) shares this opinion."

"It is more than probable that you saw correctly," Allan cried, "because a woman was mixed up in the affair of last night. Perhaps his Highness and you have not yet heard about it?"

Yussuf Khan, who had become interested and had been leaning on his elbow on the couch while he listened with wide open eyes to the story of his teacher, shook his head and the venerable Ali said:

"Colonel Morrel Sahib gave himself little time for anything else but depicting my lack of good qualities and telling me how I should atone for them. Then he hastened away to the Home Secretary for India to persuade him to grant a stay of sentence in the punishment he had intended for me. Colonel Morrel Sahib has a good heart."

Without robbing the old court poet of his opinion of Colonel Morrel's actions, Allan related what had happened the evening before. He threw a veil over the Colonel's libations, but made a strong point of his attack on the door.

They both listened to him as though he were a storyteller in some Eastern bazaar. Allan had hardly finished when steps were heard in the corridor and the door was opened. It was Colonel Morrel himself accompanied by Mr. van Schleeten.

The venerable Ali arose from his seat, with an anxious look.

"What success did you have, Colonel Morrel Sahib?" said he. "Will his Excellency, the Home Secretary for India forgive us, or are we to be driven from the city like horse-thieves?"

Colonel Morrel hesitated a moment before answering, meanwhile looking sternly at the Maharajah and the old court poet. At last he spoke slowly as though he were a headmaster lecturing two disobedient pupils:

"I have had a very difficult task. I found his Excellency

the Home Secretary for India, my highly esteemed friend," (Allan remembered having heard this gentleman referred to by Colonel Morrel under another title) "in a most excited frame of mind. The views he expressed about what—what had happened, and to which I unfortunately could not wholly take exception, the fears he entertained about what those in highest authority would say and think, the opinions which unhappily had appeared in the press—all this had affected his state of mind to such a degree, that I feared my task would be insurmountable. Only by making use of all my powers of persuasion, only by repeated appeals to our old friendship, and only by solemnly promising that the departure of your Highness would take place at once, did I succeed in persuading his Excellency to change his decision. I am accordingly able to report, that we can leave undisturbed, if we take our departure not later than the day after to-morrow. A steamer leaves for Bombay at three o'clock that day."

While the venerable Ali made a deep salaam and tried to grasp his hand, the Colonel wiped his brow, exhausted by the strenuousness of his speech and then resumed with an entirely different tone:

"Now I have done what I could for your Highness. And now it is your Highness' duty to do as you see fit with this gentleman. It depends on you what shall be done with him."

The Maharajah, who had clapped his hands after the Colonel's speech, and, strangely enough, did not seem at all disappointed at having to leave Europe so suddenly and give up all dreams of a white princess, turned to Mr. van Schleeten.

"Why, it is the jewel expert!" he cried. "How far have you proceeded in your work on the stones?"

"I. . . I began my work day before yesterday," stammered Mr. van Schleeten, "and with the Colonel's permission. . ."

"My permission was for you to work on the jewels," roared the Colonel, "not to drag in a tricky baggage, who drugged you and tried to steal them!"

"I. . . I found yesterday that I needed help in order to finish the work as quickly as possible as your Highness desired. Unfortunately my choice fell on an unsuitable person. . ."

"A saucy young baggage, whom you were love with, who administered chloroform to you as though you were on an operating-table and would have stolen everything in sight if luck and this young man had not come to the rescue! Out with it!" yelled the Colonel. "Remember, we are not at all sure but what you knew only too well what she was!"

Mr. van Schleeten cast an angry glance at Allan on the principle of being angry at others when we ought to be angry at ourselves.

"It is of course possible that the Colonel was right," he muttered, "but I can state for a fact that I saw this young man arrested at a railway station in Germany hardly a week ago. Who knows what he. . ."

"You ought to be ashamed of yourself," shouted the Colonel, "bringing up such a cock-and-bull story a second time. You know it is mere stuff and nonsense. Don't try to deny it!"

"Unfortunately it is not mere gossip, Colonel," said Allan, and related in a few words what had happened to him on the train. "I fell a victim to one of Mr. Mirzl's schemes. But what Mr. van Schleeten should mention is that it was on that occasion he became acquainted with the lady of last night. I myself was a witness to it. And there can be no doubt about the fact that the acquaintanceship was part of her plans, not to mention those of Mirzl. In some way or other they had found out about the commission Mr. van Schleeten had in London, and had decided to be prepared for any opportunities which might offer themselves. Mr. van Schleeten fell into the trap, which is easily enough understood, as the lady in question played her cards well and was unusually beautiful."

"Did she have blue eyes?" asked the Maharajah. "And blonde hair? Ah, that I must return to India so soon!" (The Colonel where he sat gave a start and stared at him.) "No, Colonel Morrel Sahib, I will go, pleased with the leniency shown by his Excellency. But. . ."

"And what does your Highness say to this affair of Mr. van Schleeten?" said the Colonel in a quiet tone of voice. "Your Highness knows that some of the jewels were stolen last night."

"Ah, a few jewels more or less!" said Yussuf Khan with a tired and dejected shake of his head. "I came to Europe for the purpose of losing my heart as the sahibs do to the white women, and all that I have lost is my good name and a couple of jewels."

"My disciple speaks well," said the venerable Ali contentedly. "His sojourn in this city has manifestly been good for him in this respect."

"Well, and Mr. van Schleeten?" insisted the Colonel, who reluctantly saw the Dutchman escaping the pillory.

"I am telling you," said Yussuf Khan, "that I envy this jewel expert, who had the good fortune of losing his heart to a woman. I have a hundred and fifty women in my palace, beautiful as gazelles and affectionate as turtle doves in early spring, but not one of them has ever fascinated me for more than an hour. To risk name and reputation for a woman, as this man has done—that must be wonderful. I pardon the jewel expert and I envy him."

"Verily," said the venerable Ali, "my disciple speaks better and better! The instructions I have given him are bearing a late but beautiful fruit. It must have been his visit to this city that has brought the fruit to its maturity."

Mr. van Schleeten, whose Bordeaux-tinged nose had kept twitching angrily during Yussuf Khan's little speech which he had been regarding as a bit of sarcasm, straightened himself up, greatly relieved after the Maharajah's last words. He began to stammer something, but Yussuf Khan prevented his expressions of gratitude by saying to the Colonel:

"There are two things which I have at heart, Colonel Morrel Sahib. One is, that a suitable reward be given to this young man, who has twice blocked those sly schemers. Will you take charge of the matter, as I am unfamiliar with European custom?"

Allan was on the point of protesting, but the Colonel forestalled him.

"A refusal would only wound the Maharajah needlessly," he said. "What would your Highness say to some of the jewels, which the young man saved from being stolen? And what do you say yourself, my young friend?"

Allan muttered something and Yussuf Khan clapped his hands.

"Splendid, splendid!" he cried. "Bring in the jewels."

A moment later for the first time Allan had the opportunity of seeing in all their glory the jewels which he had helped to preserve for their rightful owner. That they took his breath away hardly expresses it. Never before had he seen, heard, or dreamed of anything like them. It was the Land of the Orient, beaming with light from the facets of these hundreds of stones, which radiated over him like the rays of the sun through a window of many colors. When he had sufficiently recovered his composure, he chose at random a couple of unset stones, but the Maharajah, who seemed to have been imbued with new life at sight of the jewels, took up a necklace of diamonds with a blood-red ruby in the center, and mounted in links of gold that seemed pale with age. As he handed it to Allan, he said:

"Take that, if you like. It is an unworthy proof of my gratitude."

"That once," the venerable Ali added, "belonged to Mahmud, Sultan of Naishapur, at whose court the Divine Tentmaker lived. It may be he has admired it around the neck of one of the sultan's favorites, and perhaps it was about this diadem that he sang."

"Just so, splendid!" said the Colonel. "And the other matter that your Highness wished?"

It was evident that the Colonel was not as fond of the poetry of the Divine Tentmaker as the venerable Ali, but it was also clear that he had been in splendid humor ever since their departure was assured. Yussuf Khan answered:

"The other is that I would speak with the man who has charge of this caravanserai. I will tell you why, when he comes. Will you give the order, Colonel Morrel Sahib?"

With his worried look renewed, the Colonel rang the bell. A couple of minutes later the manager of the hotel appeared, having been summoned by an attendant. He began congratulating the Maharajah on his convalescence. The Colonel interrupted him:

"His Highness and suite will leave day after to-morrow!"

The manager raised a thankful glance to heaven, as he bowed.

"Not so much haste, Colonel Morrel Sahib!" said Yussuf Khan. The manager, frightened, stopped short in the middle of his bow. "Not so much haste! We leave day after to-morrow, thanks to the graciousness of his Excellency, the Home Secretary for India, but before that there is something I wish."

He turned to the manager:

"Doubtless you have some sort of hall where festivities can be held? A hall with room for many guests, such as I saw in the House of Joys?"

The manager acknowledged having such a place.

"Good. Then hear what I wish. This hall shall be made ready for a function to-morrow night, and everything shall be as like as possible to what we have in India. Since I cannot see more of the land of the sahibs, I will show the sahibs what my own land is like. It is my wish, then, that everything shall be as like what we have in my own country as it is possible."

The manager bowed deeply.

"To this function," continued Yussuf Khan, "which shall be like the festival at a Maharajah's wedding, it is my wish that all those be invited who have been subject to any unpleasantness during my sojourn here."

He made a gesture to all who were present. Allan murmured to the Colonel:

"Then the Bowlbys should be invited."

"What did the young man say?" Yussuf Khan asked.

"It seemed to him that an American family, from whose apartment the first attempt at robbery was made, should be invited," said the Colonel.

"They shall be asked," said Yussuf Khan without hesitation. "And the man who owns this caravanserai?"

The manager explained with a bow, partly that it was impossible for him to be a guest at his own hotel, and partly that he could not by any stretch of imagination be included in the category of persons who had experienced unpleasantness through his Highness' presence. The presence of his Highness at the hotel, had on the contrary. . .

Yussuf Khan stopped him with a motion of his hand. The Colonel interjected grimly:

"And Mr. van Schleeten!"

"Of course, the jewel expert as well," said Yussuf Khan. "Envied by all, that man shall sit at the banquet table, he who could lose his heart to a woman."

Mr. van Schleeten bowed, but no joy over the part he was to play at the festive board reflected itself from his Bordeaux-tinged nose. The venerable Ali on the other hand exclaimed:

"My disciple is speaking better and better and more poetically! His sojourn in this city, which, thanks to Colonel Morrel Sahib we shall be permitted to leave unshorn of our turbans and with our heads undefiled, has manifestly been good for him in this respect."

CHAPTER X

WHICH PERHAPS ATTAINS ITS PURPOSE OF CONFUSING THE READER

In London's northwestern wilderness of bricks, not far from Maida Vale, lies a brick canyon called Chesterton Mansions. As a matter of fact, with tall, steep, cliff-like brick walls of equal height, it calls to mind nothing so much as the celebrated gorges through which the rivers of Western America have eaten their way. Why it has been given that name is unknown; usually we think of mansions as surrounded by trees, but if this had been the case with Chesterton Mansions, then only the name has remained as a rudimentary indication. The seven-storied houses on the street are built as apartments, two to each floor, and since the reputation of the street is not of the best, it often happens that many of the apartments are vacant. During the month of September, when the events here related occurred, house No. 48, for example, containing apartments numbered 659 to 672, was still unoccupied as late as the eleventh of the month. But on the twelfth, a gentleman introducing himself as Baron de Citrac came to the agent and stated he wished to secure quarters where he would be as little disturbed as possible. He said he had come to London in connection with some scientific work and had brought his wife with him, for whom he would greatly prefer separate accommodations directly opposite his own. The agent, Mr. Markham, hastened to show him house No. 48. The Baron immediately decided on apartments 661 and 662, one flight up, paid his rent in advance, and requested the agent to fit up both places with plain but substantial furniture. Expressing his appreciation of Mr. Markham's obliging disposition with a five-pound note, which made Mr. Markham his slave for life, he then departed.

On Monday the fifteenth he moved in. The agent was present himself and found occasion in one respect to change his views regarding his new tenant. He had accepted the Baron's talk about scientific work simply as a poor pretext for something entirely different, something for which the French, sad to relate, are famous, and which was not unfamiliar to Chesterton Mansions: an escapade with a pseudo-Baroness. He changed his ideas on this subject when he saw the Baroness de Citrac, for although she certainly was beautiful and piquante, with gray eyes and reddish-blonde hair, yet at the same time she looked so aristocratic and haughty that the agent stood with his hat in his hand as long as she was present. The Baron, who had two servants with him, expressed his satisfaction at the furnishing of the apartments and then dismissed the agent.

The agent, who lived in one of the cross-streets, did not see his new tenant again until the sixteenth, but then under circumstances which made him once more doubt the seriousness of Mr. de Citrac's scientific studies. On the evening of the fifteenth of September Mr. Markham had attended a party which continued until a rather late hour; an unmarried friend of his, who was in business around the corner from Chesterton Mansions, had invited him to a birthday celebration. The party had begun at the Red Lion in Maida Vale, and after closing-time at this popular establishment had been continued at the bachelor quarters of his friend. The principal refreshment had been Irish whisky, and Mr. Markham was fully conscious of the effect of this drink on a person's equilibrium, when he wandered home around half-past three in the morning. He went by way of Chesterton Mansions for the simple reason that his legs seemed to entertain an inexplicable attraction toward that thoroughfare, yet without showing any marked partiality for either the one or the other side of the street; and he had just moored himself alongside a lamp-post on the left-hand sidewalk, when the stillness of the night was broken by something else than the reveille-like rat-a-tat of his heels on the flagstones. An automobile came whirring into Chesterton Mansions and stopped at the house directly opposite Mr. Markham's lamp-post. Mr. Markham's wandering gaze had just established the fact that it was house No. 48. Now he saw two gentlemen with coat collars turned up alight from the automobile and with great difficulty lift out two others, who seemed to be in a considerably worse condition than Mr. Markham himself. As a matter of fact, they couldn't stand on their legs. Mr. Markham thought he noticed that they were dressed in some sort of eccentric costume. The contrast between the oscillations of these four gentlemen and his own secure position by the lamp-post filled him with such satisfaction that he gave utterance to it in a hearty burst of laughter.

"Seem—hic—to have had e-enough," said Mr. Markham.

The lamp under which Mr. Markham stood had already been extinguished, and he did not attract the attention of the four gentlemen.

The chauffeur jumped out and took charge of one of the two gentlemen who had indulged in too much refreshment, while another of the party, the one who had first stepped out of the automobile, opened the door to No. 48. The man whom the chauffeur was propping up, gave a lurch and dropped a white turban, which rolled away on the sidewalk.

"B-been to a ma-masquerade," said Mr. Markham. "S -seem really to have had e-enough already. But they'll keep the ball a'ro-ro-rolling, of course."

The door was now open and a difficult transportation began which Mr. Markham watched with great amusement. At last the chauffeur returned alone, closed the door and drove away in the automobile without having seen Mr.

Markham.

"M-must have got a g-good big tip," said Mr. Markham with a significant laugh and slipped his moorings from the lamp-post. He had proceeded as far as the next street-corner, before he again came to anchor, and then for the purpose of airing some thoughts which had been working their way through his mind.

"F-forty-eight, the deuce!" said Mr. Markham. "The Ba-baron's apartments. The only ones—hic—rented! Scie-scientific work, ha, ha, ha! L-Lord help me, scien-tif-fific work!"

He gathered all the diversions he could from these reflections before he loosened his hold of the lamp-post and continued his unsteady journey homeward.

Mr. Markham's memory was of that enviable character, which functions even on the mornings after Irish whisky. Accordingly he recollected next morning the four gentle-men, whom he had seen going into the house No. 48, and this incident did not strike him now by morning light as being quite so humorous as it had seemed the night before. Only the chauffeur had come out of the house again; the three gentlemen then had remained overnight with the Baron? In that case, it was certain they had made a racket, and had disturbed the night rest of the people next door. During the forenoon Mr. Markham looked in at No. 46 so as to find out about the matter from the Baron's neighbor.

He was a Jew, who loaned money privately and who always arose with the sun in order to be ready to make the most he could from his debatable profession. He had arisen that morning at half-past five, he explained to Mr. Markham, but not at all on account of any noise from the house next door. On the contrary, he had scarcely heard a sound from there, but at six o'clock he had seen a gentleman with his coat collar turned up leave No. 48 and go down toward Sutherland Avenue.

"One?" asked Mr. Markham. "Only one, Mr. Streptowitz?"

"Only one," Mr. Streptowitz assured him in the melancholy tone which his voice always assumed when mentioning such a small figure.

"Only one!" repeated Mr. Markham, "but I saw four go in, and therefore three should have come out again, if the Baron was one of the four."

"The other two must have gone on before," said Mr. Streptowitz, in a sad voice as though he wanted to indicate that both gentlemen had gone to another world.

Mr. Markham admitted Mr. Streptowitz was probably right, and then went away.

That same afternoon he saw the Baron and Baroness. They stood on the landing in front of the open door to her apartment, and were holding an animated conversation in a low tone of voice. Mr. Markham, who was going up the stairs for the purpose of inspecting the vacant apartments, and who, according to his custom, wore rubber soled shoes, came within hearing distance of them without their noticing him. He caught a few words of what the Baron was saying:

"That cursed young Swedish whippersnapper! This was his night, but day after to-morrow I am planning we will take our revenge through you. . ." He caught sight of Mr. Markham and stopped short.

Mr. Markham, who thought to himself that one of the members of the night's orgie—probably the gentleman who wore the turban—must have been a Swede and had evidently been a source of annoyance to his host, gave the Baron a quiet smile as he greeted him. He thought of making some subtle allusion which would show that he knew what he knew about his tenant's scientific studies, but gave up the idea out of respect for the Baroness.

It was not until Friday, the nineteenth of September, that he had occasion to think again of the occupants in No. 48. Early that morning he happened to go past Mr. Streptowitz's apartments. This gentleman was standing in the doorway in his shirtsleeves, smoking his pipe. When he saw Mr. Markham he took his pipe out of his mouth and beckoned to him.

"They have now left 48," he said with a voice of sorrow.

"Left? Has the Baron left?" stammered Mr. Markham.

"I don't know about that, but the two gentlemen who you said were missing the other day, have gone."

"What do you mean, Mr. Streptowitz?"

"The two gentlemen who were missing the other day. You remember you said you had seen three strange gentlemen go in and I had seen only one come out. This morning at half past four, while I was dressing, I saw them leave in an automobile accompanied by another gentleman. They looked like Hindoos and seemed to be dead-drunk. It was hardly daylight then. I always get up early on Fridays, as people need money for the Sabbath."

"Hindoos, and they had remained until now!" cried Mr. Markham. "And dead-drunk at half-past four in the morning! That is scandalous, Mr. Streptowitz."

"It is," admitted Mr. Streptowitz in a slightly more cheerful tone of voice than heretofore. "At five it is time to get up and work, not be drunk. What does the Baron in number 48 do?"

"Studies," cried Mr. Markham with a shrill laugh. "Scientific work, Streptowitz! Lord help me, scientific work!"

"That is sad!" said Mr. Streptowitz. "Very sad. You will find out there is something queer about him, Mr. Markham."

Mr. Markham, who remembered the five-pound note, energetically declared that his tenant was above all suspicion.

Somewhat later the same day, a matter of business necessitated his calling on the Baron. Up to this time Chesterton Mansions had been equipped only with gas. There was now talk of supplying electricity, if the tenants so desired. Mr. Markham rang the Baron's bell in order to make the proper inquiries. As no one answered at the Baron's apartments, Mr. Markham rang the Baroness' bell. To his surprise, it was the lady herself who came to the door. She only opened the door wide enough to see who it was. She seemed wearied as though she had been keeping watch all night; her gray eyes were not as calm and cold as usual, and Mr. Markham noticed that they had black rings around them. Mr. Markham stated his object in calling and mentioned that he had rung the bell to her husband's apartments.

"My husband has gone out," she said curtly, but then immediately changed her tone, "has gone away, I mean. He has gone to Oxford in connection with his work."

Mr. Markham, who remembered what Mr. Streptowitz had told him about the three gentlemen, who had left in the morning, stared at her and indulged his curiosity.

"Has the Baron had visitors?" he asked.

She raised her brows. "What do you mean?"

"Someone saw three gentlemen leave here very early this morning," Mr. Markham stammered. The Baroness looked him straight in the eyes.

"The Baron left this morning with the servants," she said shortly. "I shall be alone in the apartments until to-morrow, but please do not let the fact be known. A woman all alone may be placed in an awkward situation."

"And the electricity?" Mr. Markham muttered, bowing humbly.

"That can wait for a day or two until the Baron returns. Good afternoon."

She politely but resolutely closed the door in Mr. Markham's face. He still stood there, staring at the door when he gave a sudden start. He couldn't swear to it but wasn't that a man's voice which he heard in the room where the Baroness was *alone*? It lasted but a moment and then all was silent. Mr. Markham gave vent to some views concerning French morals which were rather incompatible with the *Entente Cordiale*, and, as he left, muttered to himself:

"Streptowitz is right. I am sure it is a queer lot there in 48."

If Mr. Markham had possessed the power of seeing through closed doors at the moment he made this remark, his opinion would have been still more justified. Mr. Markham's ears had not deceived him; it was the voice of a man which he had thought he had heard in the Baroness' apartments, and what it had said just then was:

"Who was it? The king of thieves?"

The voice came from a young man lying on a sofa. His skin was brown and he had a short mustache; he bore traces of high living, and his eyes were encircled by black rings. These might be the result of dissipation or perhaps of privation, for the young man lying there on the sofa was bound hand and foot and was also held fast to the sofa by a girdle loosely drawn over his breast. The Baroness quietly seated herself in an armchair as the prisoner on the sofa repeated his question:

"Was that your husband, the king of thieves?"

She shook her head.

"You are persistent in your manner of expressing yourself," said she. "How many times must I tell you that the man you call the king of thieves is not my husband?"

"But you both live here together."

"No, I tell you. We each have our own apartments. His is opposite mine, and the man who just rang was the agent who has charge of the apartments. He came on a matter of business. Aren't you thirsty now? Shall I give you some lemonade?"

The prisoner on the sofa knit his brows angrily.

"I would no more accept anything from you than from him, who you say is not your husband," said he. His voice trembled with suppressed indignation. "You both have heaped an ineffaceable disgrace on my name, and indeed have shattered the plans which I had in coming to this accursed part of the world."

"But I tell you it will take at least two days before you can be set at liberty. You will either die of starvation or of thirst."

"Better that, than to accept anything from you."

The young woman bowed her head.

"As you please," she said. "Perhaps you can live two days without humiliating yourself so deeply. I understand people in your country can be buried alive and not die. But a little lemon and water need not be regarded as salt and bread."

The prisoner lay with closed eyes and did not answer. She continued slowly and as if talking to herself:

"When you awoke to consciousness a few hours ago, you drank two full glasses and you seemed to like it."

He opened his eyes and stared at her.

"Is it true or are you lying so as to catch me in a trap?"

"I am an adventuress," she said, "but I won't lie to you. Not even to draw you into some trap."

He stared at her without replying. At last he said:

"An adventuress—what is that?"

She raised her eyebrows. "How shall I explain it? I was married, my husband died, I was tired of the life I knew and I started out to find something new."

"And you found it?" His voice was eager, but without its earlier tone of excitement.

"I found at least a new kind of man," said she.

"Whom? The king of thieves!"

"Yes; he was unlike any other man I had ever met. Through a mere whim he could do some foolish thing, which might cost him his life and liberty, and then he could throw away all he had won for some other whim, more foolish than what other people could even imagine in their dreams."

The prisoner on the sofa stared straight ahead and murmured:

"I, too, was weary of the life I knew and started out in search of something new, something I had not known before."

She smiled.

"But that you have undeniably found!"

"What I sought was a woman, whose like I had never seen before."

She smiled again.

"And I suppose I was looking for that kind of man."

He stared at her in contempt.

"And you were satisfied with a king of thieves!"

"It is worth being some sort of king," said she.

"And you, who are fit to be a queen, wherever it might be, are satisfied with being the queen of thieves. By the Prophet, I cannot believe my senses."

"You are very complimentary," said she. "You would probably not be quite so polite if I told you that unlike other queens I do not content myself with letting the king reign alone. Last night I tried to make good where the king failed three days before. You have probably yourself solved the question as to why you are here."

"For the sake of a number of colored stones. The white sahibs never think of other than profit."

"A number of rather exceptional colored stones," she interposed. "But colored or not colored, they would have proved of value to me only through the consciousness that I had succeeded where the king had failed."

"Your husband! The man you love!"

"No, I tell you!" She stamped on the floor with her black satin shoe. "One who aspires to my hand, nothing more. Let me relate what he has done and what I have done, and then tell me who, up to now, most deserves the throne."

While she twined her fingers in and out, looking now and again at the sun as it disappeared behind the brick horizon of Chesterton Mansions, turning her hair into a golden reddish crown, she began to talk. The prisoner on the sofa listened to her in silence, the look in his eyes expressing in turn every emotion from contempt to admiration. After a while she stopped and looked at him, with eyebrows questioningly raised above her gray eyes. He kept silent a moment before he said slowly:

"And all for the sake of a few colored stones! If I were free, they should be yours this moment."

She leaned forward a little in her chair.

"Do you mean what you say?" she said. "Could you give away jewels whose value is above price, and to a person who has done everything to deprive you of them? Bah—you talk like other men, simply for the sake of coining pretty phrases."

He looked at her with a gaze at once both intense and tired.

"You cannot believe such a thing possible," said he, "for you belong to the race of the sahibs. In my country riches and precious stones count only for what they are, but what a man does counts for everything. But you are of the race of sahibs and to you it seems unthinkable that I, through a mere whim, would cast away that which to you is the chief aim of life."

She rose from her chair and glided toward the sofa, where he was lying.

"What would you do if I were to remove your bonds now?" said she.

He looked at her with the same tired calmness in his eyes.

"Does my promise tempt you?" he asked. "You wish to

discover whether a king's word is a king's word, even when it concerns a hundred and fifty jewels?"

Her eyes flashed and she took a couple of steps back.

"You might give me the stones now, and I would throw them in your face," said she. "If I had succeeded last night and had obtained your jewels for the possession of which I have travelled many hundred miles, I would have done the same with them. Take my word for what I say. As much as you are a king, am I a queen."

He made an attempt to raise himself from the sofa, but the bands hindered him and he fell back. He gazed at her long and steadily as though to convince himself of the true value of her words. She remained standing, looking at him with the same light still in her eyes and with the same slight raising of her upper lip. At last he said slowly and almost humbly:

"I have been blind. Forgive me! You are what you said you were, and my throat is more dry than a desert. From your hand I will accept all you will give, like the beggar his alms."

She gave a slight start; a smile played quickly on her lips, and she hurried across the room to a table where glasses and bottles stood. In a moment she was beside him again with a glass which he emptied in a single swallow. He sank back on the sofa; she pulled her easy chair a bit nearer, and sat down. They continued to measure each other with their eyes and at last he said:

"Tell me more about your life. Did you really travel

several hundred miles to obtain possession of my jewels? Without even desiring them for the sake of their value?"

She bowed her head.

"It seems to me," he said slowly, "as if I would have travelled much further, oh Maharaneeh, to meet you."

* * *

The next afternoon when Mr. Markham called at the Baroness' and Baron's apartments, no one answered. Mr. Markham rushed next door to Mr. Streptowitz. The broker nodded in confirmation.

"Yes, she has gone. I saw her go myself. But she was not alone."

"Not alone? Was she with the Baron?"

"No," said Mr. Streptowitz, "with a Hindoo. The house must be full of Hindoos. I am sure they are anarchists. And this Hindoo and the Baroness were smiling at each other like a pair of lovers."

And this was the last Chesterton Mansions saw of those illustrious personages, the Baron and Baroness de Citrac.

CHAPTER XI

A FESTIVAL AND ITS TERMINATION

I t was Allan who received the commission to present Yussuf Khan's invitation to the Bowlby family, partly for the reason that the Maharajah and the venerable Ali were not yet sufficiently firm on their legs to leave the royal suite, and partly because Allan as a personal friend of the American family seemed best suited for the mission. He therefore called on them the same evening and informed them of the invitation.

A discussion followed. Mrs. Bowlby had scarcely heard him to an end, when she flew up from her chair and declared what she would rather do, than be part and parcel to any such affair.

"Don't you think I see through him? He wants us to rehabilitate him in society after the whole town has been talking about him on account of that scandal of yesterday! That is what he wants."

"But he is leaving day after to-morrow, Mrs. Bowlby."

"And how about the princess he wanted to find?"

"He will have to give that up, and to tell the truth, he seemed to take the matter very lightly. I expected protests, but the Colonel won him over as easily as could be. The only thing he said which pointed toward regrets was his envying Mr. van Schleeten, who had succeeded in losing his heart to a woman. He himself had never succeeded in that, although he had a hundred and fifty who were ready to steal his heart from him."

"That is so like men! Ha, ha! He sits and boasts of his successes with the poor creatures and then tells how unresponsive he is himself. He ought to have a hundred and fifty lashes on the soles of his feet, that's what he should have!"

"You won't go, then, Mrs. Bowlby?"

"Why, I would rather even go to that Place where you and he were celebrating the other night."

"I will ask his Highness, and perhaps he'll hold the affair there instead."

"Now, impertinence, young friend. Helen, my child, I hope you do not for a moment desire to go."

"I would be glad to go, Mamma, awfully glad."

"And I think I'll go even if no one else does," said Mr. Bowlby.

Mrs. Bowlby had scarcely time to give vent to one sole cry of consternation, when Allan diplomatically drew something from his pocket—the necklace he had received from Yussuf Khan that same afternoon. Mrs. Bowlby stopped short in her cry.

"Mr. Cray, where *did* you get that? I thought Mirzl stole

all your money!"

"The money of mine which Mirzl appropriated would have been insufficient to pay for even the gold in which these precious stones are set. The Maharajah gave it to me to-day as a slight token of gratitude for having twice succeeded in forestalling Mirzl and his pack. Would you like to look at it?"

Mrs. Bowlby's hand flew out greedily and rapaciously like a parrot's snatching claw. She let the jewels trickle through her fingers.

"Wonderful," she whispered. "And he gave it to you? And you saw his other jewels?"

"He gave it to me. It once belonged to a Persian Sultan, the venerable Ali said. It was the Maharajah who made the choice for me. It would have taken me a year to choose among his jewels. All that I ventured to take were these unset stones."

"Opals! They bring bad luck!"

"Who knows? Perhaps they will bring me luck—what is an ill wind to sensible people often proves a favorable one to me."

"And what were the others like?"

"Bid me describe a rainbow, Mrs. Bowlby. I know only one way you can get some idea of them, that is to come to the Maharajah's function."

"There? Never! I would sooner—are you going there, John?"

"Yes, Susan dear."

"And you, Helen, you will follow me, won't you?"

"Yes, Mamma, if you go with Papa. A true married couple should always remain together, is what we were told at school."

Mrs. Bowlby gave a sigh, which seemed to show only moderate conviction on her part.

"Well, tell the Monster I will come," she said. "But I insist on Dignified Behavior. And what should one wear, Mr. Cray?"

* * *

Evidently Yussuf Khan must have modified his orders, or perhaps London had been unable to meet his requirements in every particular, for it was not altogether an Asiatic scene which met the eyes of his guests—the Bowlby family, Mr. van Schleeten and Allan—when they filed into the big banquet hall at the Grand Hotel Hermitage on the following evening, and were received by Yussuf Khan, the Colonel and the venerable Ali. The Colonel, Mr. van Schleeten, Mr. Bowlby and Allan were in evening dress, Miss Bowlby in tulle, décolleté, and Mrs. Bowlby, determined that the Stars and Stripes should stand high on this occasion, wore a gown of green and black brocade, with a train as long as herself, and was adorned with her finest jewels. Yussuf Khan and the venerable Ali were in full Oriental costume, white, wide flowing garments, each with a turban on his head. Yussuf Khan's turban bore an aigrette of diamonds, white with the exception of one lone black stone, which blazed like a lake of fiery pitch. Above his right ear hung a cluster of emeralds which drew an involuntary oh! from Mrs. Bowlby's lips. Yussuf Khan received his guests with a deep salaam.

"Welcome, my guests for the evening!" said he. "Welcome to this festivity. I trust you will accept my thanks for your willingness in honoring this occasion with your presence and I beg you to forgive the preparations being wholly unworthy of your notice. Before we go to our humble repast, may I request, Colonel Morrel Sahib, that you present those of my guests whom I have not yet had the pleasure of meeting."

While the Colonel attended to the introductions, Allan found time to look about him.

The banquet hall of the hotel was so constructed that it could be arranged according to Yussuf Khan's wishes. In style it rather resembled the interior of a temple, with very broad pillars along the sides, which bore the weight of a not particularly high ceiling. At present the ceiling as well as the walls and floor were hidden by enormous heavy Teheran rugs of fantastic pattern, which, at least in Allan's mind, gave an Asiatic effect to the broad greenish-blue marble pillars. From the ceiling draperies curved softly downward, supported in the middle of the hall by ten long lances, and beneath the baldachin thus formed, the low banquet table was spread. Around the table, instead of chairs were veritable mountains of pillows. At the side of each place was a low metal stand bearing a bowl of green porphyry. The mode of lighting was a compromise between European illumination and an allusion to the religion of the Prophet; electric lights, which together formed a huge moon-like crescent, extended from one end of the drapery-clad ceiling to the other. Like a corresponding crescent, the black body-guard, with scimitars in their belts, stood in a semi-circle around the place where the Maharajah was to sit, and here the pillows were piled somewhat higher than they were for the others. Finally, with a start, Allan noticed in a corner some semi-nude dancing-girls with golden bangles on arms and ankles. They carried broad, grotesque string instruments, and glittering tambourines. What would Mrs. Bowlby say to that? He turned his attention from the dancing girls in time to hear this lady remark to Yussuf Khan:

"I want to say that I hesitated before accepting your—" (it was noticeably difficult for her to accustom herself to his title) "your Highness' invitation."

"And why?" said Yussuf Khan. "Did the young sahib, who rescued my jewels, present my invitation in such a clumsy manner?"

"No," said Mrs. Bowlby, "but I was afraid that, as the affair was to be like affairs in the native land of your—your Highness, I—hm, might see things that a respectable woman is not accustomed to see."

"It is true," said Yussuf Khan, "in my country women of the higher class do not attend functions given by men."

Mrs. Bowlby let fly at this Oriental candor. Like a flash she forgot both ceremony and title for matters which had been on her mind for a long time.

"And in my country," she shouted, "no respectable man has a hundred and fifty wives!"

Yussuf Khan seemed to think a moment.

"But have I not heard," he said earnestly, "that a woman can have a hundred and fifty husbands, one after the other, if she makes the effort?"

Mrs. Bowlby stared at him.

"Let us shake hands," she said at last. "You caught me there. Demmit, I had never thought of that!"

"Every country," interjected the old court poet, "has its customs which a few miles from its borders already seem ridiculous and incomprehensible. This should teach us to remember that we all are nothing but playthings in the hands of Fate, as the Divine Tentmaker has so well expressed:

> *The Ball no question makes of Ayes and Noes,*
> *But Here or There as strikes the Player goes;*
> *And He that toss'd you down into the Field,*
> *He knows about it all—HE knows—HE knows!"*

He repeated a line to himself in a language that was strange to Allan and which sounded to him like "O dánad O dánad O dánad O"

Colonel Morrel hurriedly interrupted. Poetry evidently was not included in his conception of *hors d'oeuvres*.

"Isn't it time we should be seated?" said he. "Your Highness knows we are leaving early to-morrow."

Yussuf Khan broke into a laugh which made Allan give a start; a person did not expect such mirth on the part of a self-restrained Oriental. But actually the Maharajah laughed so that he showed all his teeth and Allan caught a glimpse of one that was entirely capped with gold. Yussuf Khan wiped his eyes and still laughing, said:

"You are right, Colonel Morrel Sahib. To-morrow this city will lose sight of me for a time. Let us be seated."

The Colonel, who seemed dumbfounded at the Maharajah's high spirits, the reason for which he evidently could not understand, shrugged his shoulders. Yussuf Khan repeated:

"Be seated!"

He himself led the way to the banquet table, and waited until all were gathered under the low baldachin, when he said:

"In my native land we do not take our repasts at a table such as this. But while planning this fête there were two things uppermost in my mind. The first was: These noble sahibs are not accustomed to the ways of my country and in the matter of dining each nation prefers its own customs."

"That is true," said the venerable Ali, "and my disciple speaks well."

"Then," continued Yussuf Khan, "I kept asking myself: What was it that caused me to bring discomfort to these noble sahibs, discomfort for which I, in but an humble way, wish to offer my apologies through this banquet? And the answer came: It was my jewels which were coveted by crafty and daring thieves. Now if my guests should see these jewels which, in spite of all, have a certain beauty, then perhaps they would better understand the craving of the thieves and thereby would easier forgive the discomfort which they themselves have undergone. And therefore. . ."

He stopped short and gave a clap with his hands.

All at once, like the mist which suddenly vanishes at sunrise in the tropics, there vanished from the banquet table where it had lain outspread, a white silken covering—how it happened none could tell—and Yussuf Khan's guests, with eyes half blinded, gazed upon the jewels of Nasirabad, towering like a pyramid in the center of the table. What a table decoration! Allan, the Colonel and Mr. van Schleeten, who had all seen the jewels before, stood silent, once more held spellbound by the fascinating radiance of the stones. But from the Bowlby family, who until now had not seen them, there came a three-fold stifled cry. Mrs. Bowlby's glance roamed from one diadem and necklace to the other, her eyes filled half with child-like consternation, half with distrust. At last, turning to the Maharajah who had been watching her with an earnest look, she pointed to the family jewels which she wore and mumbled:

"Please wait a moment, your Highness. Allow me to run upstairs and remove these."

Yussuf Khan gave a majestic wave of his hand.

"That would be foolish and we lose time," said he, without entering into any attempt at paying compliments. "Let us take our places."

He motioned to his guests to be seated. At his side he placed Mr. and Mrs. Bowlby; then Allan and Miss Helen, followed by the Colonel, Mr. van Schleeten and the venerable Ali. He himself was the last to sit down, at the same time raising his right arm toward the baldachin. Immediately serving-men, their black skins shining, arose from all sides, seemingly from nowhere. They filled with perfumed water the porphyry bowls at each guest's place, and put before each and every one a goblet filled with a rose-colored beverage.

"This is sherbet," said Yussuf Khan. "Later will come such refreshments as the sahibs love, but to welcome my guests I chose the drink of my own native land."

He raised his glass with a majestic movement and emptied it.

"May this humble repast help you forget the discomforts you suffered on my account!"

At the very moment he put down his goblet, a shower of roses descended over table and guests, and in the background of the hall, the dark-skinned dancing girls began a whirling dance, accompanying themselves their strange instruments. While Mrs. Bowlby jumped up from her cushions to gaze at them, Allan bent over to Miss Helen, who sat with dreamy eyes, as though she could not believe herself awake, and said:

"His Highness seems to fear no further attacks on his precious stones, since he spreads them out here in this manner."

"Why, he has his body-guard about him," said she, without taking her eyes from the pyramid on the table. "But you seem to have great respect for that man Mirzl!"

"I confess that I suspect him wherever there are two or three people together, and there is anything in the vicinity worth stealing."

"Then he ought to be in this room now," she laughed.

Allan gave a start at these words so lightly spoken by Miss Bowlby. What was it he had noticed earlier in the evening? And what was that other incident he had been trying to recall?

Yussuf Khan, who had been earnestly observing Mrs. Bowlby, said:

"It is indisputably true that some of those dancing girls, which the owner of this caravanserai has furnished, are not lacking in charm. But I for my part am far more charmed with your daughter, who seems to have reached a marriageable age."

Mrs. Bowlby uttered a cry like an angry parrot and turned her back on the dancing girls, who were whirling around in a cyclone of naked limbs and glistening gold.

"Helen," she called, "do not listen to a word of what he is saying!"

"No, Mamma."

"You ought to be ashamed of yourself!" continued Mrs. Bowlby to Yussuf Khan. "You ought to be so ashamed that you couldn't look a person in the face. You with your *hundred and fifty* women, whom you call wives, should be ashamed to lay snares for my poor innocent child!"

"Those hundred and fifty women," said Yussuf Khan, "have already been in my palace for a long time. Besides, they could be sent away, if necessary. Perhaps it is easier to love one woman than a hundred and fifty."

Mrs. Bowlby grabbed her goblet of sherbet as though she were going to throw it at his head, staring at him, utterly dumbfounded. Yussuf Khan continued as calmly as ever:

"My dynasty goes back forty-eight generations, and of my palace and wealth, these jewels bear testimony, insignificant as they may be. Had the jewel-expert who sits at the left of my teacher, not lost his heart to a woman, a thing which all should envy him, then these jewels would have had another and more attractive appearance."

"Helen!" shrieked Mrs. Bowlby in a voice choked with anger, "Helen, don't listen to him!"

Miss Helen was on the point of making some sort of answer, and the black serving-men were just appearing in festive procession, like a row of silver, with platters and dishes borne on high, when an idea suddenly struck Allan. What he had been trying to remember from earlier in the evening had come back to him and with it an idea—it seemed crazy, but. . . ! Leaning behind Miss Helen he bent over to Colonel Morrel. He whispered two questions to the Colonel which made the latter stare at him in utter astonishment, until finally he seemed to regain his power of speech.

"What in Tophet do you mean?" he roared. "Have you

completely gone off your head?"

Allan rose from his seat.

"What do I mean?" he shouted, looking at Yussuf Khan with flashing eyes, "I mean that by no manner of means is the man sitting there Yussuf Khan, Maharajah of Nasirabad!"

He had scarcely hurled this remark, when a pounding was heard on the door leading into the banquet hall. It flew open, and three strange figures appeared on the threshold.

First came the man, who had said he could not be present at an entertainment in his own establishment—the manager of the Grand Hotel Hermitage. Then came a woman, at sight of whom Mrs. Bowlby gave a jump as though she had seen a rattlesnake, and then a person in crushed and wrinkled clothes and rather soiled collar, who bore a certain resemblance to the Maharajah of Nasirabad.

CHAPTER XII

THE MARRIAGE OF YUSSUF KHAN

I t was the manager of the Grand Hotel who broke the silence which was caused by his entering the banquet hall, accompanied by the two others. He turned to Colonel Morrel and with an apologetic emphasis on each word he uttered, said:

"Colonel, you must excuse me for forcing myself into your presence. You must understand it did not happen without pressing reasons. I will state what has occurred as briefly and plainly as possible.

"Twenty minutes ago I was called to the office with the explanation that my presence there was absolutely necessary. I hurried down and found this lady, whom I recognized as the Mrs. Langtrey who had stopped at the hotel some time ago, and this gentleman, who bears a certain resemblance to his Highness." (The manager made a bow in the direction of Yussuf Khan). "I could not believe my eyes, when I saw Mrs. Langtrey, who as we know, made a bold attack on his Highness' jewels two days ago, concerning which one of his

Highness' guests of the evening should be able to furnish complete details." (The manager made a slight bow to Mr. van Schleeten, who was sitting as rigid as though he had had a stroke, his eyes riveted on Mrs. Langtrey.) "Before I could express my astonishment, Mrs. Langtrey said: 'I know precisely what you are going to say. It is unnecessary. I am the Mrs. Langtrey who was stopping at your hotel; this is the Maharajah of Nasirabad, who was kidnapped five days ago.'

"'How dare you say that this person is the Maharajah,' I exclaimed, 'when I know that the Maharajah is at this very moment giving a farewell banquet in my hotel!'

"'The Maharajah!' answered Mrs. Langtrey. "A fine sort of Maharajah. The fellow who is giving the banquet in your hotel to-night is no more Maharajah than you yourself or the porter there. I demand to be shown to the banquet-hall immediately.'

"This was too much for me and I was thinking of calling the attendants to remove Mrs. Langtrey from the hotel, when she anticipated me by saying, 'Don't do anything which you will regret later! We would prefer not to call on the police for help, but if it becomes necessary we shall do so.' After that statement I considered there was nothing left for me to do but escort these people up here as they demanded."

The manager stopped. The Colonel stared about him like a dazed person, now at the manager, now at Allan, now at the two claimants to the throne of Nasirabad. The last of these to put in an appearance, the man who came with Mrs. Langtrey and wore the wrinkled coat, began:

"How long must I wait before this thief in my image is thrown into chains?" said he. "For five days I have been in his hands and those of his accomplices, and when I return and find he has stolen my name, if not my possessions, I am treated as though *I* were he. Colonel Morrel Sahib, how long need I wait before this criminal is thrown into chains?"

The Colonel, with eyes wandering in astonishment from him to the Maharajah seated at the table, was unable to utter a syllable. He had known the Maharajah for many years; at the table sat a Yussuf Khan whom he remembered from a thousand different occasions, in the center of the floor stood a person with sunken cheeks and wrinkled clothes, who bore a certain resemblance to that other Yussuf Khan, but nothing more. But that coincidence of this young man from Sweden, boldly breaking out with an absurd statement almost at the very moment when the same assertion was made in such a peculiar manner from another source! He still stood there utterly confused, when the silence was broken. The Maharajah at the table was starting to speak, but Mr. Allan Kragh discourteously interrupted him.

"Colonel Morrel," said he, "a short time ago I asked you two questions, which you then considered the ravings of a madman. Have I your permission to repeat them?"

The Colonel nodded stiffly, doubtless without even thinking of what Allan said, so utterly dumbfounded did he seem as he continued to stare at the two pretenders.

"I asked you," said Allan, "whether his Highness the Maharajah ever had any occasion for dentistry work being done in Nasirabad. Will you give me an explicit answer this time?"

The Colonel turned to Allan with a stare, the dumbfounded look still in his eyes.

"Dentistry work," he roared, "this is neither time nor place for such idiotic nonsense."

"Perhaps it is not as idiotic as you think," said Allan. "From your reply I draw the conclusion that his Highness had nothing done to his teeth in Nasirabad. Had he been to the dentist in London?"

"Now, look here, my young friend. . ."

"All right. Then, neither in London. Now I happen to know that the person sitting at that table has a tooth in his lower jaw crowned with gold. If he can disprove it, then one of my reasons for insisting that he is not the Maharajah of Nasirabad falls through. I hereby give him the opportunity of immediately proving my statement to be false."

Yussuf Khan arose from the table, his eyes flashing.

"I know nothing about hospitality among the sahibs," he said, "and the courtesies due them as hosts. But if anyone in my country spoke to me, his host, as this young man has, I would let my servants drive him with blows and lashes from my house. Am I a horse, that on command I should open my mouth for examination? Let them be driven out, these people whom I do not know, and who have forced themselves in here like impudent beggars, and with them, this young man, who has insulted me as I have never been insulted before."

He looked at Allan and the unbidden guests with eyes flaming with rage. The Colonel straightened himself up, and was on the point of doing as requested, when Allan, a faint smile on his lips, checked him with a slight movement of his hand.

"Colonel Morrel," said he, "just a moment! I will gladly let myself be driven out, as his Highness desires and in the manner he wishes, but only on one condition. I think Mrs. Langtrey and the person with her will also agree on their part when they hear what my condition is."

He turned to the Maharajah at the table:

"Benjamin Mirzl, Commander of the Faithful and King of all Criminals, will you yourself kindly give the orders to your black body-guard that I should be driven out! I have the pleasure of knowing that they do not speak English!"

While Allan was speaking an expression, terrible to look upon, came over the Maharajah's features. He left his place by the table and with measured steps approached the group near the door. He kept his eyes fixed on Allan, eyes that glistened like those of a royal tiger. He stopped in front of Allan and for a moment pierced him through and through with a look of such fierce anger that the Colonel started forward to interfere, expecting to see him strike Allan down on the spot. At that instant, however, something entirely different happened. The Maharajah, with one gigantic spring, was past them all, a spring not unworthy of that royal beast of prey, which he so resembled: before a soul could make a move, the hall was dark as pitch; they heard the door slam and the rattle of a lock as the key was quickly turned. For a moment all was wild confusion; there were cries from Mrs. Bowlby, from the Colonel, the black body-guard, the manager and from the unbidden guests who had arrived but such a short time before. Then came a shout of satisfaction from someone who had succeeded in finding the electric switch and the hall was ablaze with light once more.

Masses of arms and legs, beating and kicking, belabored the door; various expressions from the Colonel, in the midst of this confusion and struggle, indicated that not all the blows reached the panels of the door. Finally the door flew open, and a wild chase started down the stairs to the large hall below. Fortunately for the future reputation of the hotel, there was nobody in the hall except a couple of attendants and the porter. With the roar of a tiger the manager fired a question at them and after a second of surprised astonishment the dignified porter with the figure of a Benedictine bottle answered:

"Man disguised as the Maharajah? The Maharajah came down the stairs a moment ago — and well, he seemed to be a bit unsteady on his legs. 'Am g-going out and get a l-little fr-fresh air,' he mumbled to us, sir, and looked at us rather unsteadily. We heard shouts from up in the banquet hall, and thought that the guests were getting in fine spirits and. . ."

The next moment they had dashed past the dignified porter. Like a pack of hounds who had picked up the scent they found the trace. As luck would have it, the trail led them no further than Monmouth Square. The policeman on duty there reported that two minutes before he had helped an Asiatic gentleman, who seemed to be a trifle tipsy, into an automobile which had then proceeded to Grosvenor Hotel, where the gentleman said he was stopping.

The Colonel looked at Allan, while he wiped the perspiration from his forehead.

"That cursed rascal," he mumbled. "The third time! And he came within a hair's breadth of succeeding. . . Devil take him and yet I can't help admiring him!"

"Let us go up again," said the manager. "His Highness. . . his real Highness, will probably be able to explain a few matters."

He, the Colonel and Allan started back to the hotel; Mr. van Schleeten had not taken part in the chase after the counterfeit Maharajah. The people in Monmouth Square stared at the three gentlemen, whose faces were dripping with perspiration, in spite of the fact that they wore nothing but regulation evening dress. On entering the banquet hall, their eyes met a motley scene.

To the left of the entrance stood the Bowlby family, presided over by Mrs. Bowlby, who with skirts outspread was prepared to defend her family like a hen her chicks. She was carrying on an animated conversation in an undertone with her husband and daughter and every now and then, with a quick glance, eyed Mrs. Langtrey from top to toe. Mrs. Langtrey stood in the center of the hall bearing herself proudly, a mysterious smile on her lips. Her eyes hung on Yussuf Khan—he who finally had been recognized as the real one—and deeply sunken on a cushion at the banquet table, with nose changed in color from Château Lafitte to Haut Sauterne, his bushy yellowish-gray mustache now loosely hanging down, sat a gentleman whose eyes saw nothing but Mrs. Langtrey—Mr. van Schleeten. The black serving men and the body-guard had flocked together in a circle, like a colony of crows, chattering about the events that had happened. Yussuf Khan (the right one) still somewhat limp and flaccid, stood with an emptied wine-glass in his hand and was the object for sympathizing words and prayers of forgiveness on the part of his old teacher.

"By the Prophet, my son, I blush with shame, like a thief caught red-handed in some bazaar! I, even I, your teacher, for two days allowed myself to be imposed upon by that most brazen of all impostors. Even his speech was yours, although more poetical, but therein I saw fruit of the instruction I had sought to impart. My pride at this (may Allah forgive my sin) made me but more blind to his real character. In truth, by the Prophet, I blush with shame! Were it not for this young man with the marvellous piercing eye of a falcon, I believe that by now you would have been driven forth, and he, the impostor, would have sat upon the throne of Nasirabad a few weeks hence, when we see again our native land for which I yearn like the deer does for the spring of cooling water. Most aptly says the Divine Tentmaker. . ."

The Maharajah interrupted him without waiting for the Divine Tentmaker's apt observation.

"Doubtless," said he, straightening himself up, "this young man, who is a stranger to me, deserves the credit for exposing him, but yet there was one with me, who was ready to unmask him. She but waited to choose the moment."

"My son, it is a source of sorrow and regret to me that you do not listen as willingly to the words of the Divine Tentmaker as did that wretched imposter, that son of Sheitan. But you said *she*? Do you mean the woman who came here with you?"

"It is as you say. It is she, who came here with me, she, who was chosen by that impostor and kidnapper to be my jailer, she who was merciful toward me during the time of my imprisonment and she, concerning whom there is a further matter I soon shall mention to you and Colonel Morrel Sahib. For five days she was my custodian, only in the beginning was she relieved by that king of thieves. Her mildness of manner, combined with firmness of purpose, was wondrous, and the days I spent in confinement while she watched over me, were sweeter to me than all the hours I have passed in the company of other women. She was as firm as the hand of a horseman when it holds the reins, and yet as tender as the same hand when it strokes the rider's mount. To-day—but more about that later. You said that within a few weeks we should see our native land again. Was the time already settled for our departure?"

"It was settled for to-morrow by Colonel Morrel Sahib, who yesterday, as a great favor, succeeded in obtaining permission from his Excellency the Home Secretary for India, that we might leave this city still in possession of our honor and our turbans. This city has never before heard of such happenings as have occurred through our presence, and both the population here and Colonel Morrel Sahib are justly indignant at me for setting my pupil such a bad example. Ah, you can in truth, apply to your teacher what the divine Omar said of his teachers:

> *Myself when young did eagerly frequent*
> *Doctor and Saint, and heard great argument*
> *About it and about: but evermore*
> *Came—"*

"Here comes Colonel Morrel Sahib," interrupted Yussuf Khan. "It is well. I will immediately speak to him about what lies nearest my heart."

He went up to the Colonel, who was still wiping his forehead after his pursuit of the impostor, and who every now and then, muttering an energetic expression, rubbed his shins, which had fared so badly in the scrimmage by the door. He stared at Yussuf Khan, with all too little pleasure at the return of the real pretender showing in his eyes.

"A pretty bit of business!" he exclaimed as if Yussuf Khan was to blame for Mr. Mirzl's misdeeds. "Did I say a confoundedly pretty bit of business? It is just a mass of confoundedly pretty bits of business! If Providence had not sent us this young man—" he pointed at Allan— "the devil only knows what would have happened."

"Who is this young man?" asked Yussuf Khan.

"He has a name which would split your tongue to pronounce but that doesn't matter. This is the third time he has thwarted that arch-swindler, who could even get the better of the devil himself if he really went about it. If they have many like him in Germany, then we ought to place a tax on everybody coming from that country. Why, this young man here—just listen!" He gave the Maharajah a short, but vivid and picturesque description of Mr. Mirzl's and Allan's three encounters, and did not neglect to weave in moral reflections about Yussuf Khan's own part in the misfortunes which had been visited on him (the Colonel) ever since his arrival in Europe, a part of the globe which blushed with shame to see such things happen before its very eyes. Yussuf Khan listened patiently until the Colonel had finished and then said:

"My teacher Ali told me, it had been your intention to depart for Nasirabad to-morrow, with this impostor as king in place of me. Is that correct?"

The Colonel growled a half angry, half embarrassed yes.

"Very well. It is also my intention to leave to-morrow. Regarding this young man, I will consider later what shall be done to show him my gratitude. But there is another matter to settle first. I crossed the seas and came to this country for the purpose of winning a suitable wife from among the sahibs' people."

"A princess!" snarled the Colonel. "We can lay that plan on the shelf, after all that has happened to your Highness here in London. White princesses are somewhat particular."

"You are speaking foolishly, Colonel Morrel Sahib. We shall not lay this plan on the shelf, as you express it. My wedding will be celebrated this very evening."

"Ha, ha! Fine! Where is the princess?"

"Here," said Yussuf Khan calmly, and turned towards Mrs. Langtrey.

Gradually all the people in the hall had gathered in a circle around him, and at his last words a piercing shriek came from where Mrs. Bowlby stood, still protecting her family behind her outspread wings of green brocade.

"Ha, ha! she to become a queen!"

Yussuf Khan looked at Mrs. Bowlby. "Who is this jabbering woman, screeching through her nose?" said he.

"Pay no attention to her, your Highness," said Mr. Bowlby. "With a nose the size of hers you can't blame her if she screeches through it."

"John! You too! You forsake your wife, and insult her publicly?"

"My dear Susan, are you becoming vain in your old age? You know your nose is a number ten. Besides, you are the guest of his Highness and you have no right to give offense either to him or to any of his guests."

Mrs. Bowlby seemed ready to explode; however, she

succeeded in smothering her feelings within her breast and held her tongue after she had made a deep but ironical curt-sey to all assembled in the circle. But yet her glance seemed to skip Mrs. Langtrey. Yussuf Khan took Mrs. Langtrey by the hand and turned to his old teacher.

"After me," said he, "comes my teacher Ali as Sheik-ul-Islam in Nasirabad. As such it is he who joins together bride and groom at royal weddings, and it is he who is best suited later to impart the teachings of the prophet to the bride."

At these words a hoarse cry, in spite of all, arose from Mrs. Bowlby's breast:

"She to become a Mohammedan! And the hundred and fifty other wives?"

Yussuf Khan again turned to her with an earnest and astonished look.

"How foolishly this woman speaks every time she utters a word! A true believer in the teachings of the Prophet may have but four wives. Personally, I have only two."

"Two! How dares he—why, the whole world knows. . ."

"The others are merely slaves," said Yussuf Khan. "All will be removed from the palace to a suitable abiding-place. Henceforward and on my return to Nasirabad, I shall have but one wife, as do the rulers of the Sahibs."

He solemnly made a deep salaam before Mrs. Langtrey, who followed his every movement with a look of tender and joyous happiness; and then turning to the manager of the hotel, said:

"Let everything be put in readiness for the wedding feast,

which will be held in my apartments. A banquet, suitable
to the occasion, shall be given there after the wedding. In
this hall, which has been defiled by that impostor, I will
remain no longer."

* * *

In spite of everything curiosity got the better of Mrs.
Bowlby's other feelings and when the wedding festival
was celebrated in Yussuf Khan's apartments at eleven
o'clock that evening, she, too, was there, by invitation of
the Maharajah, who listened to all she had to say with the
same interest and astonishment as he would pay to a parrot
which had learned to talk. The banquet was held this time
in European fashion. The jewels of Nasirabad were securely
locked in the mahogany chest and placed in charge of the
black body-guard, well protected from any further attack
on the part of Mr. Mirzl. The only bit of Oriental color
was the venerable Ali, who, in Eastern costume, chanted
in honor of his disciple a solemn nuptial hymn which suffered somewhat from the fact that Pommery brut had been
served in rather liberal quantities. Mrs. Langtrey celebrated
her last evening in European dress with a modesty which
even half appeased Mrs. Bowlby. Yet, as the opportunity
arose, this lady could not resist drawing the Maharajah
aside, and asking:

"But doesn't your Highness know, that your Highness'—
hm—wife has been married at least once before?"

"What does that matter to me?" said Yussuf Khan. "I,

too, have been married at least once before."

It was difficult for Mrs. Bowlby to dispute this fact.

"And that she was on friendly terms with the man who made three attempts not only to steal your Highness' jewels, but even your Highness, too," obstinately continued Mrs. Bowlby, who hardly seemed able to believe her own ears. "And that she herself—"

"I know it all. What is that to me? She is eyes and ears to me. What I have never seen I shall see through her, and what I have never heard, she will tell me. Never have I passed through days sweeter than the last two, when she was my custodian and during our talks together gradually became something else and who chose me in place of that man, who had aspired to her hand and who had appealed to her through his daring. Perhaps, he, through his courage, was worthier of her than I, who even otherwise am unworthy of her. In no woman's company have I tasted such happiness as when she gave me food and drink and finally loosened the cords that bound me. Her will is firm as a blade of steel and yet yieldingly soft as the down on the breast of a dove. And above all else, she is my Maharaneeh."

The affair had been in progress an hour, when the manager appeared at the door of the Maharajah's dining-room, bowing deeply and presenting a silver server on which lay two telegrams. The Maharajah was not sufficiently familiar with European customs at a wedding to understand the meaning of this procedure, but Colonel Morrel hurried forward to receive the telegrams. He opened one of them, stared at it a moment, and then turned red with anger. He was on the point of throwing it away, when Yussuf Khan stopped him.

"What is written on that piece of paper?" said he. "I wish to know. Does it refer to me?"

The Colonel cleared his throat.

"It is a telegram from that swindler," he muttered.

"Good, let us hear it. Although the man is an impostor, yet he certainly has courage. Let us hear it, Colonel Morrel Sahib."

The Colonel read:

> *To the Royal Bridal Couple, Grand Hotel Hermitage.*
>
> *Unworthy congratulations from the fallen pretender, May the rightful heirs continue to flourish and multiply! Tell her Majesty that I understand it may seem more interesting for a woman to rule over fifteen million men than over only one, who perhaps alone outweighs the fifteen million, and that it may seem more honorable to continue the line of Nasirabad rulers than the family of de Citrac!*
>
> *BENJAMIN MIRZL, ex-Maharajah,*
> *ex-Baron de Citrac*

"And the other?" said Yussuf Khan, who had listened to the Colonel with unruffled earnestness.

"It is for the young man with the unpronounceable name."

"For me!" shouted Allan. "I can well believe I would be remembered. Read it, Colonel Morrel."

"If you wish it," said the Colonel, who opened the telegram, and then read:

> *Mr. Allan Kragh, Suite of the Maharajah of Nasirabad, Grand Hotel Hermitage.*
>
> *You have thwarted my plans three times, but I am not angry with you. It was I myself who fell into the trap. Like Mr. van Schleeten, I let myself be deceived by a woman. For three years I tried to win her hand, and then she rejected me so she could rule over fifteen million men. Just one bit of advice: Do not let us meet a fourth time!*
>
> *MIRZL.*

Allan's private interview with the former Mrs. Langtrey, which took place a short time later, was brief and consisted only of a smile and a pressure of the hand.

CHAPTER XIII

SINGLE TICKET, NASIRABAD

T here is a deep-rooted conviction among old imbibers
that no after-effects are so severe as those from
champagne. Allan Kragh was not unwilling to subscribe to
this view on the morning after Yussuf Khan's marriage.

As a matter of fact, his position was hardly a comfortable one. It was true he had been through adventures,
adventures like in A Thousand and One Nights, adventures
as intoxicating as champagne—but this morning what he
felt most of all was their after-effect. Mr. Mirzl had run
off with his funds, and he did not yet know whether the
hotel would reimburse him. It was pretty certain Mr. Mirzl
would not. Yussuf Khan had made mention of rewards for
the services he had rendered the ruler of Nasirabad, but
after a somewhat indefinite remark in that direction, he had
allowed the evening to pass without any further reference
to the matter. To be sure he had the necklace belonging to
the Nasirabad crown jewels, but since he had received this
from Mr. Mirzl during the latter's brief reign, he evidently
could do nothing else but return it. And even if he should
be reimbursed by the hotel, what should he do then? After

the adventures he had been through, the majority of experiences would seem dull and uninteresting. Go back home? The very thought of the clamoring creditors at home made a shiver run down his back such as the gladiators of old felt at thought of the hungry lions in the arena. Well, in the first place, he might as well go to the manager, anyway, and ask him what the prospects were for his being reimbursed for the money which had been stolen.

The manager evidently was suffering from the same champagne-like after-effects as Allan, due to his own experiences of the day before. His manner was distant, and he did not seem to be in a very obliging mood.

"As I told you, I cannot settle the matter myself. Of course I appreciate all that you have done, if not for the hotel, then at least for one of its guests, but as I said, I cannot promise anything definite before I have talked the matter over with the directors."

Allan shrugged his shoulders and then was wandering about the hall when he suddenly remembered that Yussuf Khan and his suite were to depart at noon, and therefore it was high time that he return the necklace he had received from ex-Maharajah Mirzl. He had deposited it in the hotel's banking department with the same young man, who once upon a time had allowed Mr. Mirzl to draw out his money. Strange to say, it was still there! But it took some time for the young bank clerk to be sufficiently convinced he was dealing with the proper person, and the difficulty in establishing his identity did not improve Allan's temper.

"Had you been half as careful that other time, I would now be richer by three hundred pounds," Allan growled at the man as he left to go upstairs. The black body-guard in the corridor, watching over their master's safety, did not seem to be suffering from the same depression as Allan. They were snickering and whispering together in their crowlike dialect; evidently they had found out they were to leave for home, and were already rejoicing at the fact. They admitted Allan with grins on their faces. They had learned to recognize him.

The old court poet was alone in the antechamber. He greeted Allan with the same cheerful smile as had the body-guard outside.

"Ah!" said he. "Within a few hours we will be on the mighty ocean, tormented by that sickness which it is customary for the demons of the sea to call forth among travellers. Yes, it will be but a few hours, and then we will leave this great and wonderful city of which, thanks to the King of Impostors, we have seen so little."

"You do not seem distressed at the idea of encountering the demons of the sea," said Allan.

"No, for they are necessary to take me back to my native land. Well and pleasantly has a poet expressed it, although one who cannot indeed be compared with the Divine Tentmaker: To those born among the palm trees, the pines seem ugly, and to the people of Delhi the stench of their city is as perfume."

"'Pon my word, excellent," said Allan. "What does

Delhi look like nowadays?"

"In truth, my young friend, I cannot tell you that. Four times ten years have passed since I visited that city. All I actually remember is a terrible stench, and a sun, such as the people of London could not dream about, even though they were to chew the hashish leaf, a sun as unbearable as the eye of Allah to the unfaithful."

"It seems to be a pleasant place," said Allan.

"My young friend," said the venerable court poet, "do I understand correctly that you have never been to Delhi?"

"You understand me correctly," said Allan. "Strange to say, I have happened to forget to pay Delhi a visit."

"But surely you have been in India," said Ali trustfully.

"I am sorry to disappoint you," said Allan, "but ridiculous as it must seem, I haven't been to India even once. I am an uneducated ass with closely cropped ears and with blinkers before my eyes. Doesn't your Divine Tentmaker say something like that somewhere?"

"The Divine Omar has never given utterance to such an observation," said Ali. "It must have been some other poet of less importance. But he who has never been in India is like an inexperienced child and he who has never been in Nasirabad is like one unborn. There the sky is of a deeper blue than elsewhere and the air is more cool. And yet the sun shines unusually clear, but it does not burn like the sun on the unfaithful in Delhi. Cedars and pines cover the mountains and in their shade is a fragrance sweeter than that from a woman's hair. Caravans, with armed escorts, wend their way up and down through the passes, and at nightfall savory odors of boiled mutton, rice and of sweet-scented butter arise from their camp fires. This is a perfume sweeter, more delicious, than all others, and he who has never known it is like a man who has never tasted wine or kissed the lips of a woman he loves. The women of Nasirabad have more slender waists, heavier hips, and smaller hands and feet than other women, and their eyes are black, glistening like night in winter. Nay, he who has never been in Nasirabad has never lived."

"I am beginning to believe it," murmured Allan to himself, and while the old poet continued to describe his native land in lengthy sentences, often quoting from the Divine Tentmaker and other poets of less importance, Allan within his soul caught a glimpse of the whole Orient with its subtle fragrance and its motley scenes, highly sparkling like the gleams of light and color from Yussuf Khan's jewels. He was still standing, half lost in his dream, when the door to the inner room opened and Yussuf Khan himself appeared, accompanied by his wife and the Colonel. Allan made a deep bow and took from his pocket the necklace, which Yussuf Khan looked at with an air of surprise.

"I received this from him who pretended to be your Highness," said Allan, "and I beg permission of your Highness to return it, before he steals it from me."

"Received it from him?" repeated Yussuf Khan.

"As a reward," interrupted the venerable Ali. "Because this young man had twice prevented him stealing your jewels, my son, the King of Impostors, as a reward, presented him with the necklace of precious stones. I myself was present at that time. This swindler's effrontery was somewhat relieved by a sense of humor, which I at times admire."

Yussuf Khan looked at Allan.

"And now you want to return it," said he. "Why?"

"I had received it from an impostor," Allan began. Yussuf Khan interrupted him:

"That doesn't matter. The King of Impostors, who wanted to steal my jewels, and who for two days stole my name, has done a deed which deserves credit. I owe you, young sahib, more than this piece of jewelry can make good. Tell me what I can do to repay you. Speak freely and be sure that whatever you ask is already granted."

Allan looked hesitatingly at the necklace he held in his hand. To accept presents and rewards was contrary to his inborn instinct, and yet he felt he would give offense, through a refusal. And at the same time he could not free his mind from thinking what should he do, when these persons had left, in whose drama he, too, had played a part. The venerable Ali said to the Maharajah:

"Think, my son, this young man, whose features bear evidence of ability and a noble disposition, and who has done us great service, has never seen either Delhi or Nasirabad. Nay, he has not even been in India. In words chosen from the best of our poets, for my ability is so far inferior that I am unworthy to compete with them, I have tried to give him a pale picture of the beauty of Nasirabad."

An idea flashed through Allan's mind which made him tremble. After these adventures, as though from A Thousand and One Nights, everything but A Thousand and One Nights would seem flat and stale. . . And could A Thousand and One Nights really be found elsewhere than in that most ancient land of tales and adventures?

"Your Highness," said he, "let me receive some position in your Highness' service in Nasirabad!"

Yussuf Khan stared at him. "Is that all you wish?" he asked.

"Yes," said Allan, "whatever the position may be."

Yussuf Khan looked at him for yet another moment.

"Good," said he. "I promised your desire should be gratified, whatever you might ask. From this day forth you shall be the one person nearest and closest to me in all matters excepting those which affect the government of the sahibs in my country. But remember, we leave this city in a few hours."

"I know," said Allan, "and I will make haste with my packing. I shall pack my bags for a journey to the land of A Thousand and One Nights!"

* * *

A couple of hours later he repeated the same words to the Bowlbys when—with his three hundred pounds which had been refunded to him by the hotel, in his pocket—he took leave of them on the steps of the hotel. Mrs. Bowlby, in a critical mood to the last, said:

"I bet he will simply put you to watch his Hundred and Fifty."

"Mrs. Bowlby," said Allan, "I fear certain qualifications, which I do not possess, are required for such a position."

Colonel Morrel, who was standing nearby, smiled grimly behind his white mustache and took occasion to add:

"All right, my young friend. India has changed a bit since the days of Harun al Raschid. There is no surety that you will meet with similar adventures to those offered in A Thousand and One Nights. But if necessary you can always obtain a position with Government and make the acquaintance of something with which I do not believe you have, as yet, had much experience—work. It is time for us to get into the automobile."

"And work," cried Mr. Bowlby as he waved a good-bye to Allan, "that, all said and done, is the biggest adventure of all!"

THE END

A Note
From The Publisher

We hope you enjoyed *Beware of Railway-Journeys,* by the first internationally famous Swedish crime writer, Frank Heller! This book was originally titled *The Marriage of Yussuf Khan* (now you've read it, you'll understand why), but this Kabaty Press edition was retitled to reflect better the contents.

Just for fun, we've made available on www.<u>kabatypress.com/books</u> a number of FREE Frank Heller short stories, featuring his recurring sleuth Mr Collin. While you're there, why not join our mailing list, and make sure you're always up to date about our upcoming releases?

The Scandinavian Mystery Classics Series

THE MAN WHO PLUNDERED THE CITY: AN ASBJØRN KRAG MYSTERY

Sven Elvestad
(trans. Frederick H Martens)

When a series of jewel thefts scandalise Christiania (now Oslo), detective Asbjørn Krag encounters a master criminal who has his measure–or does he? From the dark brickyards on the city's outskirts to the bright lights of the Grand Hotel, Krag must use all his skill to turn the tables on the gang and their mysterious leader.

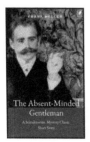

THE ABSENT-MINDED GENTLEMAN: A SCANDINAVIAN MYSTERY CLASSIC SHORT STORY

Frank Heller
(trans. Robert Emmons Lee)

When a counterfeiting ring rocks London, the trail leads to a curiosity shop and a professor offering a treatment for 'absent-minded gentlemen'–but can Detective Kenyon get to the bottom of the clever scheme?

THE GRAND DUKE'S FINANCES
(Upcoming in Autumn 2022)

Frank Heller
(trans. Robert Emmons Lee)

The Grand Dukes of the tiny island of Minorca have been happily bankrupt for generations. But when the current Grand Duke is threatened by blackmail, and a band of revolutionaries takes over the island in his absence, the situation looks bleak – until he crosses paths with Mr Collin and a mysterious woman under his protection.

Lightning Source UK Ltd.
Milton Keynes UK
UKHW010156070223
416581UK00003B/195